MONTANA MAVERICKS

Welcome to Big Sky Country, home of the Montana Mavericks! Where free-spirited men and women discover love on the range.

THE REAL COWBOYS OF BRONCO HEIGHTS

The young people of Bronco are so busy with their careers—and their ranches—that they have pushed all thoughts of love to the back burner. Elderly Winona Cobbs knows full well what it is like to live a life that is only half full. And she is determined to help them see the error of their ways...

Oh-so-handsome cowboy Jameson John knows he's considered a "catch," but he's never wanted to be caught...until now. His one-night stand with Vanessa Cruise over the winter was meant to be no strings attached. Now, however, he's mesmerized by brainy, beautiful Van, and she doesn't want to change the rules!

Dear Reader,

Welcome back to Bronco, Montana. It's summertime, and here in Big Sky Country, we do the Fourth of July up right. It's called Red, White and Bronco, and it's a four-day festival celebrating Independence Day.

Born and raised in Bronco, high school science teacher Vanessa Cruise left town brokenhearted nine years ago. She's returned now and then to visit her family, but she's vowed to never again make Bronco her home. Yes, it's true that this year she's here for the whole summer, teaching summer-camp science to tweens and early teens. But come fall, she's returning to Billings and the good life she's made for herself there.

Rancher Jameson John is a Bronco man through and through. No way would he ever live anywhere else. In his younger years, Jameson was something of a player. And Van has a weakness for players—somehow, they always end up breaking her heart.

Well, not this time, Van promises herself. She's powerfully attracted to Jameson, but no way will she allow herself to fall in love with him.

Jameson, however, is determined to convince his disaffected hometown girl to give love one more chance—with him. And on the second of July, at the Miss Bronco Beauty Pageant, something totally unexpected is about to happen, something that will give Jameson the romantic opportunity he's been waiting for...

It's a great year for love here in Bronco. I hope Jameson and Vanessa's story tugs at your heartstrings and reminds you that love is stronger than all our fears and doubts.

Happy reading, everyone!

Christine Rimmer

The Rancher's Summer Secret

CHRISTINE RIMMER

HARLEQUIN

SPECIAL
EDITION

Special thanks and acknowledgment are given to Christine Rimmer for her contribution to the Montana Mavericks: The Real Cowboys of Bronco Heights miniseries.

HARLEQUIN®

SPECIAL EDITION™

PLEASE RECYCLE

Recycling programs
for this product may
not exist in your area.

ISBN-13: 978-1-335-40792-4

The Rancher's Summer Secret

For questions and comments about the quality of this book, please contact us at CustomerService@Harlequin.com.

Harlequin Enterprises ULC
22 Adelaide St. West, 40th Floor
Toronto, Ontario M5H 4E3, Canada
www.Harlequin.com

Printed in U.S.A.

Christine Rimmer came to her profession the long way around. She tried everything from acting to teaching to telephone sales. Now she's finally found work that suits her perfectly. She insists she never had a problem keeping a job—she was merely gaining "life experience" for her future as a novelist. Christine lives with her family in Oregon. Visit her at christinerimmer.com.

Visit the Author Profile page
at Harlequin.com for more titles.

For MSR, always.

Chapter One

Last New Year's Eve

Jameson John fully intended to ring in the New Year in style.

He wanted to hear some good music, play a little eight ball and, if the stars aligned, take someone sweet and willing home. To make all that happen, he'd jumped in his quad cab and headed straight for Wild Willa's Saloon.

Perched on Center Street, with the entrance in Bronco Valley and the dance floor in tony Bronco Heights, Wild Willa's was the most popular bar in Bronco, Montana. At Wild Willa's, things got loud and rowdy pretty much every night. On New Year's Eve, however, the fun reached a whole new level.

As midnight approached, the very air seemed charged with anticipation. The sound of boots stomping on hardwood competed with the wail of the fiddle, the beat of the drums and the driving rhythm from the bass guitar.

Tonight, every man wore his best boots and a snap-front dress shirt. Every woman had on her tightest jeans or her shortest flirty skirt. Many wore light-up, sequined cowboy hats. They blew party horns and shouted encouragements at the band. The place smelled of beer, perfume, saddle soap and sweat.

"Hey, cowboy, let's dance."

Jameson turned to the pretty blonde who'd just tapped him on the shoulder. She had lipstick on her straight white teeth and a woozy look in those big blue eyes. Like just about everyone else in Wild Willa's tonight, she'd had one too many.

As for Jameson, in the two hours since he'd walked through the wide, rustic double doors, he'd had a whiskey, neat, and a single beer. He wanted to be sharp, on his best game, just in case he met someone interesting. So far, that hadn't happened. It wouldn't be happening with this cowgirl, either.

But the woozy blonde looked sweet and hopeful. He gave her a smile and led her out on the packed dance floor.

When the song ended, another cowboy stepped up. Jameson thanked the blonde and left the floor. He tried not to feel discouraged, but at this rate, he'd have nobody to kiss when the clock struck twelve. Maybe it just wasn't his night.

With a shrug, he decided he needed a second whiskey and a seat at Wild Willa's famous Get-Lucky Bar, which formed four loops of stools in a four leaf clover configuration.

Too bad every stool had an occupant. Jameson considered heading for the pool tables. He could order a drink there.

But then, in the split second before he turned for the tables, a guy at one end of the clover got up. Jameson moved in to claim the seat.

"Good luck, buddy," muttered the other man as he went by. He looked kind of glum, like maybe he'd just been shut down.

Jameson slid onto the vacant stool, with the wall on one side and a curvy brunette on the other.

He signaled the nearest bartender and ordered, "Knob Creek, straight up."

The brunette turned a pair of velvet brown eyes his way—and he almost felt sorry for that other guy. But then her wide, plump lips stretched in a devilish smile.

The rich, musical sound of her laughter had him forgetting all about that other guy. "Well, if it isn't the one and only Jameson John." She raised her glass as the bartender set his drink down. "Hot and handsome as ever, I see."

Suddenly, his evening looked a whole lot more promising. Apparently, this gorgeous woman knew him. He studied her more closely.

She did look a little familiar. He raised his whiskey and tapped the glass to hers.

"Wait—don't tell me," he said. "I know that I know you…"

She laughed again, tossing her head, her thick, wavy hair tumbling down her back, gleaming like polished mahogany. He found himself staring at the smooth olive skin of her throat. "I'm Vanessa," she said. "Vanessa Cruise."

"Wow." He never would have guessed. Tipping his hat to her, he said with frank admiration, "Evan Cruise's little sister grew up."

Vanessa had always been cute and smart, but somewhere along the line she'd turned into a beauty—the natural kind, in a silky white shirt and a pair of snug jeans that hugged every gorgeous, generous curve. She had that thick dark hair, those fine eyes to match and freckles, too. Everything about her appealed to him.

She shook a finger at him. "You are staring, Jameson John."

"Sorry, can't help it. I like your freckles."

"Now, there's an interesting compliment."

"Freckles seem surprising, somehow, with your skin color."

"It's a fallacy that only redheads have them. You know that, right?"

He liked her voice—kind of low, husky. "Tell me more."

She laughed. "It's just a reaction to UV exposure. A result of the overproduction of melanin."

"Well, I like them on you. If I remember correctly, everyone used to call you Van, right?"

"Van or Vanessa, either way."

"Just checking. I really like Vanessa. It suits you better, somehow. Didn't you move away?"

She gave a slow nod. "I live in Billings now."

"A teacher, right?"

"You remembered."

"English?"

"Science—chemistry and biology."

"That's right. Always a brainy one."

"You'd better believe it." Her thick, dark eyelashes swept down and up again.

"Home for the holidays, huh?"

She leaned closer. "It's my last night in town. Tomorrow I head back to Billings." Her shoulder brushed his arm, and his breath caught. She smelled sweet and fresh, like the roses his mother grew beside the steps of the main house out at the family ranch, the Double J.

"Vanessa." He touched the brim of his hat, a salute meant to signal he held her in the highest regard. "You mind if I ask you a personal question?"

"Go for it."

"Got a guy in Billings—someone who can't wait for you to come home?"

She sipped her drink. "Not now, I don't."

Something in her tone alerted him. "Did I just hit a nerve? I didn't mean to—"

"Not your fault." She waved his apology away with a shapely hand, the nails cut short, businesslike. No-nonsense. Her full, tempting breasts rose and fell as she sighed. "I confess. There was someone, yes. I was *trying*, you know?"

"I don't quite follow. Trying to…?"

"What can I tell you? This someone I just mentioned wasn't my type, but my type kept messing me over. I go for the players and that never goes well. Trevor—that's his name—was no player. I met him at a science fair. He was so nice. Nerdy and shy, you know? I felt zero chemistry with him. But chemistry isn't everything, am I right?"

He stifled a chuckle. "Vanessa, I'm not touching that with a ten-foot cattle prod."

She let out another soft sigh. "I thought I could draw him out, get him to relax and have fun. I thought that he would be true to me and I would slowly come to care for him deeply, to be grateful for his steady ways."

"I have to say it. Trevor sounds dead boring—and let me guess. You finally had to face the fact that Trevor wasn't the guy for you?"

She seemed faintly amused. "Not exactly."

"Then what?"

"Just before I came home for Christmas, Trevor dumped me."

He couldn't believe it. "No way."

"Oh yeah."

"Trevor is a damn fool."

She leaned close again. The scent of roses beckoned him as she whispered, "He said he couldn't be with me anymore because he didn't find me sexually attractive."

Jameson knew he must have heard wrong. "What man with a pulse wouldn't be attracted to you?"

She grinned. "Yeah, well. You win some, you lose some, I guess."

From over by the pool tables, some guy let out a whoop and someone else whistled. Applause followed. The band struck up another song, this one loud and fast.

When the noise died down a little, she asked, "You here with a date?"

"Nope. Just having a drink with a fascinating woman."

She studied his face for a long count of five before declaring, "You're playing me, aren't you?"

He sat up a little straighter. "No, I am not. Trevor blew it, and I'm grateful to that clown. Because if he hadn't, you wouldn't be sitting here next to me on New Year's Eve."

Slowly, she turned her glass on its Wild Willa's coaster, the one that showed a sexy cowgirl in a short skirt riding a bucking bronc and waving her red hat above her head.

"What?" he asked low. "Say it."

"You are bad," she observed. "So. Very. Bad— and I like that about you far too much."

"Being bad is good, then?" he asked hopefully.

"Oh yes, it is. In the context of this moment, of you and me side by side on New Year's Eve at the Get-Lucky Bar, being bad is very, very good."

As the band struck up another fast one, they gazed at each other, eye to eye. Time passed, but neither of them looked away. He saw no reason to speak. He could just sit here beside her, staring into those sultry eyes of hers until next year came around.

Except he really did like the sound of her voice, especially when she kept those eyes on him and spoke to him alone.

He asked about her family.

And she brought him up to speed on the Cruises. Her brother, Evan, owner and operator of Bronco Ghost Tours, had just gotten engaged earlier that night to Daphne Taylor, estranged daughter of the richest rancher in the county. Vanessa's mother had a boyfriend now, and Vanessa's grandmother Dorothea, whom the Cruise family called Grandma Daisy, had recently found out that *her* mother was not her birth mother.

"That is some big news," he observed.

"And there's more."

He couldn't wait another second to touch her. Prepared to apologize profusely if she slapped his hand away, he guided a thick curl of hair behind the perfect shell of her ear. She didn't object. Instead, a tiny smile pulled at one corner of that mouth he hoped he might get to kiss when midnight rolled around.

"Tell me everything," he commanded.

"Well, I'll tell you this. Grandma Daisy's birth mother—*my* great-grandmother—is *the* Winona Cobbs."

"Wait. You mean Winona Cobbs who wrote the famous 'Wisdom by Winona' syndicated column?" He used to read that column every week. Winona Cobbs gave good advice.

"The one and only."

"Lots going on with you Cruises." Things never got that exciting on the Double J.

Lowering her voice and leaning closer to him once more, Vanessa confessed, "I feel a little bit guilty. I ran out on tonight's family New Year's Eve party at Daphne's Happy Hearts Animal Sanctuary." Daphne Taylor was somewhat famous locally—not only for being the only daughter of cattle baron Cornelius Taylor, but also for not eating meat in the middle of cow country *and* for her rescue farm, where she took in every brokedown horse and runaway goat that wandered by.

"Please don't get me wrong," said Vanessa. "I'm glad Daphne and Evan found each other. And my mother, who's in love with her boss, is happier than she's ever been before."

"But?"

"It's just that seeing the people I love all cozily coupled up only makes me more depressed about my own romantic future—plus, well, the family doesn't exactly know that it all blew up with Trevor."

He pretended to look stern. "Holding out on the family. That's just not right."

"Maybe not." She drew her shoulders back. "But I don't feel up to dealing with their loving concern at the moment, if you know what I mean." She looked sad.

And he felt bad for teasing her. "I was just yanking your chain. Honestly, I hear you. Sometimes the people you love are the last ones you want in your business."

She braced her elbow on the bar and propped her pretty chin on the heel of her hand. "Thank you." She seemed to mean it.

He nodded in acknowledgment. "And I want you to know that your secret is safe with me."

"Good." Her expression changed, and he had no idea what she might be thinking as she warned, "And *you'd* better watch out."

"Why is that?"

A slow grin curved that mouth, which was so damn inviting it probably ought to come with a warning. "I'm in a mood to forget all my troubles, and I have a weakness for players like you."

Wait, he thought. *Players?*

He was no player—yeah, okay, maybe he'd come here tonight in hopes of meeting someone like her. And maybe, back in the day, he'd dated a lot of different women.

But since then, he'd grown up. He'd been married and divorced. He was older and wiser now, a man who'd learned enough about what mattered in life to want more from a woman than a one-night stand.

However...

Apparently, Vanessa Cruise *liked* players. He didn't want to mess with the program if she might be considering making his night.

"Vanessa, Vanessa," he chanted under his breath.

"Hmm?"

"You're so direct."

She frowned. "Is it too much?"

"I like it."

Her frown smoothed out. She signaled the bartender.

How many had she had? It mattered. No self-respecting man took advantage of a woman under the influence.

The bartender stepped close. Vanessa said, "Another club soda with lemon." Jameson felt relief—and Vanessa must have seen something in his face. "What?"

"You're not drinking."

She gave him a half shrug. "I'm my own designated driver—and if I do get lucky here at the Get-Lucky Bar, I don't want my senses dulled by alcohol. I want to be wide-awake and fully functional when things get thrilling, you hear what I'm saying?"

Did he ever.

She nodded her thanks at the bartender as he set her club soda in front of her. After that, she stared down into the drink for a second too long.

"Hey," he said gently, and brushed a hand down her arm. "Where'd you go?"

Her soft shoulders slumped as she blew out a breath. "Just tell me the truth. Am I ridiculous?"

"Hell, no." He said it with feeling. "Whatever gave you that idea?"

She looked at him sideways, kind of pooching out her lower lip, looking a little bit pouty and so damn cute. "It's hard on the ego, being dumped for a complete lack of sex appeal."

Jameson felt nothing but outrage on her behalf. "Don't talk like that. Your ex was the one with the problem."

"As in, it's not me, it's *him*?"

He stuck to his guns. "That's right. You're way too much woman for Trevor."

She sipped her drink. "Just hypothetically…"

"Hypothetically, what?"

"Well, say we went home together…"

"I'm liking the sound of this."

She bit the corner of her ripe lower lip before asking sheepishly, "Would you tell me if I was bad in bed?"

Where the hell did that Trevor guy get off, making her doubt her desirability? Mr. Nice Guy was nothing but a jerk. "It's not an issue. You aren't bad in bed."

"Jameson. Get real. You have no way of knowing that."

They were leaning into each other again, close enough that his sleeve touched hers. It was a simple matter to lean in the necessary fraction closer.

Their lips met.

Her mouth was even softer than it looked, and the scent of her was driving him a little bit crazy. He kissed her slowly, his body heating with sexual need, though he exercised care not to take it too deep. "That proves it," he whispered, his lips still brushing hers. "You are amazing in bed."

Her slow-blooming smile foreshadowed really good things. "Tell me you live alone."

"I'll go you one better. I'll show you." He signaled the bartender for the check.

Van's butterflies had butterflies as Jameson settled the bill, helped her into her fleece-lined coat and led her outside, where a light snow was falling.

Wrapping a strong arm across her shoulders, he pulled her in close to him. "Ride with me."

No way. Tonight would be her first—and most likely only—one-night stand. She intended to do it right. And that meant sober, with her own vehicle to get her there and, when the night was over, back to her brother's house, where she was staying alone while Evan stayed at Daphne's.

"I've got snow tires on my SUV," she said. "I'll follow you."

Jameson didn't argue. He walked her to her Subaru, opened her door for her and closed it with care. She watched as he jogged through the thin layer of snow to a black quad cab. Starting her engine, she waited for him to take the lead.

He led her out of the parking lot and down Center Street to the intersection with the state highway, where dirty snow had piled up on the shoulder, but the road itself was clear. The snow came down sparsely, not really sticking.

After maybe ten miles, he took a side road. A few minutes later, they turned onto a wide, well-tended gravel driveway and passed under a rough-hewn sign for the John family ranch, the Double J. In the distance, she could make out the shadows of barns and outbuildings and a big log house. Jameson led her past the turnoff to that house.

The long driveway curved up the gentle slope of a hill and then down to another house, one not quite as large as the log home they'd passed earlier. Of gorgeous, weathered wood and stone, the house had lots of windows and a more modern style than the usual sprawling log homes that most of the wealthy local ranchers favored.

Two of the four garage doors rumbled up and Jameson drove in the first stall, jumping out and signaling her to take the next stall over.

She rolled down her window. "I'll just park out here." When it came time to leave, she wanted a clean getaway, one that did not include asking him to please shut the garage door behind her.

He went in through the garage, and she parked in the driveway, meeting him at the front door.

Inside, he took her coat and hung it in the entry closet. "Drink?" he asked, leading her down a wide hallway with a skylight overhead. The hallway opened onto a sprawling, gorgeous combination kitchen and great room. The kitchen end had a stone floor, counters of black granite and warm wood, the appliances the kind any top chef might envy. A wall of windows looked out on the dark, shadowed peaks of the mountains in the distance.

"Nothing for me, thanks," she said, setting her leather shoulder bag on one of the stools at the granite island.

He pulled her over to the rough-hewn trestle table and moved in close. Really, he was such a gorgeous man. She'd always admired his thick, dark gold hair and celestial blue eyes. He smelled so good, like saddle soap and clean leather—a healthy male in his prime, the kind that lured a woman to mate.

And that reminded her. "I'm on the pill," she announced, "and really hoping that you have condoms."

Had that come out sounding painfully abrupt? Maybe. But it had to be said. A woman needed to take responsibility for her safety and reproductive health. No surprise pregnancies—and no STDs, either.

"Yes, I do." He took her hand. His was warm and thrillingly rough from ranch work. Her heart skipped a beat with anticipation. "This way," he said in a low rumble.

He led her out of the kitchen area to the open great room, which had a high, peaked ceiling and more gorgeous skylights. Large, comfortable-looking sofas and chairs formed two conversation groups on either side of the plain, modern fireplace.

Across from the fireplace, a staircase with metal railings led down to other rooms below.

"This way." He led her along the short hallway next to the staircase, where a door opened on the master suite, with its own large bathroom and private deck. The room had a peaked ceiling, too. It was all warm, rough-textured woods, the linens in soothing, soft grays.

She hesitated at the door. He stopped and turned to her.

Before he could wrap her in those big arms, she stepped back. "I have something I need to say."

He lifted a hand and touched the side of her face. The simple caress thrilled her, sent a tingle rushing through her just from that small, brushing contact. "Tell me, then."

She suddenly felt awkward and silly and...too young. But she said her piece anyway. "I just need to lay out the ground rules, so we both know where we stand."

One side of his sinfully sexy mouth quirked up in amusement. "There are ground rules?"

She gave him a firm nod. "Yes, there are. This, tonight, is a special circumstance."

"Very special," he agreed, those beautiful eyes gleaming at her, promising all manner of heavenly delights.

"Well, that may be. But I meant special as in a onetime deal. Tomorrow, I head home to Billings."

"You mentioned that already."

"And it bears repeating. I live in Billings, and your life is here. And in future, when I come back again to visit my family and you and I happen to see each other somehow in passing, we will not stop. We will not give each other more than a nod and a simple hello. We will never discuss what happened here tonight. No digits will be exchanged. Neither of us will try to contact the other. This is 'The Night That Never Happened'—" Yes, she actually air-quoted it for emphasis. "—and we need to agree that it is."

His burnished eyebrows drew together in a doubtful sort of frown.

She barreled on. "Which, er, won't be a problem for you because you don't do relationships."

"Vanessa, I never said—"

"Wait." She put up a hand. "I won't get in touch

again because that would make you think I want a relationship, which I don't. As for you, well, you won't contact me because, um, you're Jameson John and you don't do commitment."

His frown had deepened. "Hey, now. Hold on a minute. I do plan to have a relationship that lasts. I want a family, children."

"Sure you do," she teased. "Someday, right?"

"That's not fair." He really seemed troubled, somehow, by this subject.

"I'm sorry," she said, and meant it. "Sometimes I get a little carried away trying to make a point. I didn't mean to insult you, Jameson."

"You didn't. It's just, well, yeah. Maybe I was that guy you're describing. But I'm not anymore. You like players and, back at Wild Willa's, I wanted to be whatever you needed tonight. But I'm not that guy, Vanessa, not the thoughtless boy you remember from high school. I've been married and divorced. I'm settled down now, a grown-ass man. I'm ready for something more than just one night."

Her heart kind of melted—but come on. She'd just been dumped. A new relationship wasn't even on the table right now and she needed to make that crystal clear. She gazed up at him defiantly. "Well, I'm not ready for anything but tonight."

He stared down at her long and hard. Was this

it, then? Would he walk her back out to her car and say good-night? She braced herself for that.

But then he shook his head. "I do want you, Vanessa. A lot. And if tonight is all I'm getting, so be it."

She drilled her point home. "After this, there will be no contact. You and me, we won't be happening again."

He caught her hand and pulled her close. "Fair enough."

"Jameson," she whispered, pressing her palms to his hard chest as his mouth touched hers.

Oh, he was perfect. Exactly what she needed. This beautiful man to ring in a whole new year, to make her feel gorgeous and wanted for one perfect night. She slid her hungry hands up to encircle his neck.

When he lifted his head, she opened her eyes. They gazed at each other. "Agreed?" she asked again.

His eyes spoke of reluctance to go along with her terms. She shouldn't allow herself to feel thrilled at the idea that he might hope for more. Yet she did feel thrilled. Just a little.

Finally, he acquiesced. "I agree. Tonight and that's all."

Gathering her close again, he shut the door to the hallway with the heel of his boot.

* * *

Much later, when Vanessa woke beside Jameson in his big, comfy bed, it was still dark out. The bedside clock showed ten past three.

A whole new year had begun—and boy, did Jameson John know how to give a girl a really good time. For several dreamy seconds, Van stared at him through the shadows. He lay on his back, sound asleep. Looking at his chiseled profile, she could almost wish that she didn't have to go.

But they had an agreement. And she intended to keep it.

Carefully, so as not to wake him, she slid out from under the thick down comforter and tiptoed around the room gathering up her clothes. In the bathroom, she dressed and finger-combed her tangled hair.

Then, carrying her boots in order not to make a sound, she crept along the short hallway and across the great room to get her purse from where she'd left it on the kitchen stool.

Her contacts were extended wear, but still her eyes felt gritty and tired. She switched to her glasses—the ones with the large, black frames.

At the bottom of her bag, she found the small notebook and a blue Flair pen she always carried with her. Tearing out a page, she wrote a brief note.

Leaving the note on the island, she headed for the entry, where she paused long enough to put on her warm coat. The front door opened silently on well-oiled hinges when she carefully pulled it wide.

Outside, the sky had cleared, and a light rime of snow made the ground glitter as though scattered with tiny diamonds. She paused on the step to breathe in the fresh, icy air.

And then, with a secret smile on her face and a lightness in her step, she turned for her Subaru.

Jameson woke alone to pale sunlight—a clear winter morning.

When he reached out a hand, the other side of the bed felt cold to the touch. He stared up through the skylight at the pale, cloudless sky and hated that Vanessa had already left him.

Rising, he pulled on last night's jeans and went out to the kitchen area to brew some coffee. He found her note waiting on the counter.

Jameson,
   I just want to say that you are incredible.
Thank you for a perfect New Year's.
Yours,
Vanessa

Two sentences bracketed with his name and hers. That's all he got.

As he crumpled the scrap of paper in his fist, he weighed the pros and cons of breaking her damn rules—right now, today. She wouldn't have left town yet. He could probably track her down at Evan's house or her mother's place on the Bronco Valley side of town.

But he'd given his word not to go after her. He'd promised to walk on by any time he happened to see her again. Plus, she lived in Billings, while he loved Bronco and the Double J. He never planned to live anywhere else.

Beyond all that, maybe she was right. She'd insisted she wasn't in the market for a relationship. And the last thing he needed was to fall for another woman who couldn't honestly, openly give him her heart—even a woman as surprising and sexy and smart and charming as Vanessa Cruise.

Jameson drank his coffee, fried bacon and scrambled some eggs. After breakfast, he went out to meet his brothers, Maddox and Dawson. Together, they rounded up some frisky heifers who'd busted through a fence and wandered out onto the state highway. That evening, he had dinner with the family at the main house.

And New Year's night, in bed alone, he stared up into the darkness and tried to picture Vanessa at home in Billings, lying in her own bed, maybe smiling a little, remembering the night before. Faintly, he smelled roses. He grabbed her pillow and pressed it to his face. Breathing in the scent of her like some sappy lovesick fool, he reconsidered the idea of going after her.

But he did no such thing. She didn't want to see him again and he'd given her his word he wouldn't track her down. Jameson John always kept his word.

Eventually, he promised himself, the desire to go after her would fade.

Chapter Two

Present day

The Night That Never Happened turned out to have a day of reckoning, and that day was July 2.

By then, due to her inability to say no to Daphne, Vanessa had been in town for a month. Her brother's fiancée had mad skills when it came to coaxing people to do things they would ordinarily have no trouble politely turning down. Things like spending the summer in the hometown Van never visited for longer than a week or two at a stretch. Somehow, Daphne had convinced her that she needed to teach science to tweens and early teens out at Happy Hearts Animal Sanctuary.

Daphne's day camp, Young Adventurers, kept a lot of kids busy in the summer while their parents worked. In the mornings, Young Adventurers offered a fun and absorbing curriculum, an opportunity to learn cool stuff about chemistry, math, technology and biology. After lunch, the younger kids could pet the animals and learn about animal behavior while the older ones pitched in on the farm. They all seemed to love summer day camp at Happy Hearts.

And truth to tell, Van loved it, too. She loved it enough that she might not even have minded spending a whole summer in the town she'd left behind—except for the niggling little issue of a guy called Jameson John.

Every day for the past month, Van had wondered and worried, dreaded and anticipated the moment when she would finally come face-to-face with Jameson again.

Yet somehow, one day had followed another and she'd seen no sign of him. She'd even started imagining that she never would.

Wrong.

That gorgeous, sunny, early July day just happened to be the opening day of Red, White and Bronco—because in Bronco, people took their patriotism seriously. Every year, the town leaders and merchants pooled their resources to put on a four-day festival in celebration of Independence Day.

Van and Callie Sheldrick, Van's summer roommate, had arrived at Bronco Park early to make sure they got a picnic table. A down-to-earth sort of person, both perceptive and warmhearted, Callie worked for Evan at Bronco Ghost Tours. She and Van had quickly become BFFs. In fact, during a girls' night, just the two of them, a month ago, Van had shared her hardest secrets with Callie.

Today, Bronco Park looked nothing short of festive, with red, white and blue paper cloths on the tables, Old Glory waving from every tree and a whole marketplace of booths selling fireworks and patriotic hats, horns, dishware and souvenirs—along with just about every kind of picnic food and drink known to man. The smells of barbecue, popcorn and cotton candy filled the air.

Maybe twenty minutes after Van and Callie claimed their table, Evan and Daphne joined them, followed by three bright young girls who attended Vanessa's morning workshops at Young Adventurers. More girls arrived—too many to fit at the table. But one of the girls had brought a blanket. They spread it out between the tables and sat on the grass.

Red, white and blue bunting graced the front

of the outdoor stage set up in full view of all the picnic tables. The festival committee had also put out rows of white folding chairs so that everyone would have a place to sit and enjoy today's main event—the Miss Bronco beauty pageant, held every year on the second of July, right here in Bronco Park.

This year, the contest had sparked controversy, thanks to several of Van's students at Young Adventurers—the ones sitting at the table with her and nearby on the grass, as a matter of fact. The girls had spearheaded a successful campaign to rewrite the pageant rules. Some people weren't happy with the changes.

Van thought it was great, and she'd shown up today to support her girls. She'd always made it a point to encourage her pupils to think outside the box. She urged them to transform what they found unfair or even downright wrong about their world and the way it was run. To that end, at Young Adventurers, she held discussion time each morning before everyone got down to work on current projects.

Back in early June, during discussion time, one of the girls had brought up the Miss Bronco pageant. She'd complained that girls from the same families almost always seemed to win, and that didn't seem fair. A lively chat ensued.

And after that, the girls had done more than

talk. They'd created a petition to change the rules and then gone door to door collecting the signatures to make that happen.

Van beamed with pride as the pageant began and Earl Tillson, this year's host, kicked things off by explaining the new contest rules.

"This year," announced Earl, "Miss Bronco will be chosen *not* by the usual panel of pillars of our community, but by an open vote to be held right here, today, as soon as the competition is concluded. Anyone in town can cast a vote as long as they fill out a ballot. Also this year, as a nod to all the single ladies you admire and want to recognize, you'll find a space on your ballot for a write-in. Any and all unmarried females sixteen years of age or older are eligible."

"Sixteen years or *older*?" A skinny cowboy in a purple shirt jumped up from one of the picnic tables. "How *much* older?"

"Well," replied Earl, "she would need to still be breathin', I'll tell you that." A ripple of laughter passed through the crowd.

That same cowboy argued, "That means any woman, no matter how old, can enter—long as she ain't got a ring on her finger."

"Young man," growled Earl, "that is exactly what it means. As long as any single female person is sixteen, which we all agree is old enough to carry out the duties of the position, that person is welcome to claim her chance at the crown."

"Well, that is plain wrong, Earl Tillson. We'll end up with somebody's single grandma wearing the sash and crown."

Thirteen-year-old Cleo Davidson, one of Vanessa's brightest summer students and an organizer in the campaign to make the Miss Bronco contest less biased and more inclusive, put her hands to either side of her mouth and shouted, "It is fair, and it is right!" Several spectators, including the girls seated around Van, cheered in support.

The cowboy bellowed, "No, it's not!"

"Yes, it is!" Cleo shouted back. "Your grandma should have the right to enter."

"Like hell she should!" yelled the cowboy. "Some old lady can't be Miss Bronco. It's a beauty pageant. I love my grandma, but she's no Miss Bronco."

Snickers and titters followed that pronouncement.

"Young man, curb your tongue!" Earl, who did a brisk side business as an auctioneer at local livestock shows and estate sales, knew how to take control of an iffy situation. He stared that cowboy down.

Muttering under his breath and shaking his head, the cowboy sank back to his seat.

"Now. Where was I?" Earl straightened his bolo tie. "Ahem. There will be no swimsuit competition." That brought some serious booing. Earl waited for the yahoos to take a breath before shouting out, "The categories of competition are talent, evening wear, an interview centering around the contestants' dreams and goals—and a platform for a social cause that has special meaning for each candidate."

Van felt so proud. Her girls had done well. She beamed at the three across the table from her and turned to give a big thumbs-up to the five sitting on the grass.

And it was right then, as she shifted her focus to the girls on the blanket, that the moment of reckoning found her.

She spotted Jameson. He sat at a picnic table on the other side of the rows of folding chairs. At the table with him, she recognized his dad, his mom and his two younger brothers.

Her mouth went dry, and her face felt too hot. She couldn't stop herself from drinking in the sight of him. He looked so good, all strong and broad and big and manly.

It seemed almost impossible that she'd actually seen him naked. But she had. And their night together had been beautiful. Perfect. Spectacular.

Yeah. All those things and then some.

But what she needed to remember, the most important thing now...

That night was Over. Capital *O*.

Just one night, she reminded herself. One night, months ago. Little more than a blip on the radar of eternity. The mere sight of him shouldn't affect her so strongly.

She was supposed to be over him—no. Wait. She had no need to get over him. There was nothing to get over. They'd had a good time and gone their separate ways.

Except, well...

For her, their one night had been the best night ever.

The sheer sexual excellence of it couldn't quite be forgotten. Her body remembered and wanted more.

And that meant that her face had flushed with heat and her mind had gone blank as a fresh-washed chalkboard. All of a sudden, a hive full of bees seemed to buzz beneath the surface of her skin.

And he'd spotted her, too.

Their gazes collided—and locked. They stared at each other across the rows of spectators as Earl Tillson droned on up on the stage. Everyone else—Callie, Evan, Daphne, the girls—they all just faded away. Her brain had only one thing in it: a tall, broad-shouldered, blue-eyed, golden-haired cowboy.

He gave her that slow smile, and she felt summoned.

She had to actively resist the desire to rise from the picnic bench and go to him, take his hand, lead him away from the crowd to someplace private where they could get up close and very personal all over again.

Not that she would do any such thing.

Uh-uh. Van stayed right there at the picnic table next to Callie.

It was just, well, she'd daydreamed about him way too often—about him and The Night That Never Happened—so much so, in fact, that she'd come to think of that night simply by its initials: TNTNH.

Van shut her eyes. Closing out the very sight of him, she ordered the bees to stop buzzing and her face to stop burning. With a slow, deep breath, she made herself look at him again. With a dignified nod and a reserved little smile, she turned away.

"So you've met Jameson?" said a soft voice in her ear.

She turned to aim a bright smile at Callie, who was watching her much too closely. "I did grow up here," she reminded her friend, who had no idea what Van had been up to last New Year's

Eve. She and Callie hadn't been that close back then. And now, well, what did it matter? Yeah, she'd shared her hardest secrets with Callie, but Jameson?

He was a *good* memory, a happy secret. She didn't need to cry on her friend's shoulder over him. Plus, Jameson was one night and nothing more.

"Of course I've met him," she said to Callie. "Everybody in town knows Jameson John."

Was that a smirk on Callie's face?

If so, Vanessa refused to acknowledge it.

When the slender, pretty blonde stepped forward from the pack of ten contestants up on the stage, Jameson tore his gaze from the hot brunette across the way. After all, that pretty blonde was his baby sister. Her name was Charity. Along with his brothers and his parents and a lot of other people in the park that day, Jameson clapped and cheered wildly as Earl introduced her.

Charity looked beautiful, as always, in a pretty summer dress, her shining hair loose on her shoulders. Jameson had shown up with the rest of the family to support her in her current bid for the Miss Bronco crown. They all knew she had it nailed this year.

Nineteen now, Charity had been working toward the Miss Bronco title every year since she turned sixteen. Each of those years she'd come closer to winning. She'd taken, respectively, fourth place, third place and runner-up. This year would bring her the crown.

She smiled her brilliant smile and gave a short speech about how she loved her hometown, had graduated with honors from Bronco High and had finished her first year at Valley College. The John family and her other supporters clapped louder than ever when Earl thanked her and she stepped back for the next contestant to take her turn.

As for Jameson, his gaze strayed once more to the unforgettable brunette at the table on the opposite side of the stage. The sight of her had decided him. He might have come today to support his sister, but now he had a second goal—finding an opportunity to reconnect with Vanessa.

Word traveled fast in Bronco. He'd known for a month that she'd moved to town for the summer. Within a week, he'd found out that she was rooming with Callie Sheldrick. He'd ached to head straight for Callie's place. He wanted to get up close and personal, to intimately welcome Vanessa back to town. He hungered to find out if the sparks between them burned as bright and hot as they had last New Year's Eve.

But he'd stopped himself from going after her. He'd reminded himself that he'd given his word not to seek her out, that he needed to stick with the promise he'd made New Year's Eve.

However, seeing her again in the flesh changed everything. To hell with her rules. He wanted to get closer to her.

And one way or another, he would.

For the next hour, he tried his damnedest to sit tight with his family, to keep his mind on the pageant. He got through the interviews, snapping to attention when his sister stepped up. Charity spoke of her dreams and goals with warmth and feeling. She went first in the talent portion and stole the show. Charity played the piano like a virtuoso and she sang like Carrie Underwood— kind of looked like her, too.

Yeah, he might be a tad prejudiced in his little sister's favor, but objectively, everyone could see that she deserved the crown. People clapped louder and with greater enthusiasm for her than the other nine contestants. Even with the new rules in place, Jameson knew she would win.

As he cheered his sister on, he kept one eye on the woman across the way. He was biding his time, waiting for the right moment. Eventually, Vanessa would get up to say hi to a friend at another table, maybe check out the rows of marketplace booths, buy herself a cold drink or some patriotic trinket. When she did, he would make his move and find a way to get a few words with her.

An hour and a half crawled by after that exhilarating moment when he'd looked over and spotted her sitting with her brother and the others. Now and then, he would slide her a glance, kind of keeping an eye on her. Once or twice, he caught her looking his way.

But she didn't hold his gaze. And that one measly, cool little smile she'd given him that first time their eyes locked together, well, that was all the smiles he got.

One way or another, he intended to get more.

Finally, she made her move, rising from the table, hovering there a minute to say something to Callie. And then she took off, headed for the two rows of marketplace booths set up facing each other farther into the park, on her side of the stage.

In order not to be too obvious, he waited until she'd made it forty yards or so from her table, before whispering to his brother Maddox, "Be right back," and setting out after her.

Up on the stage, wearing a determined expression and dressed in a sequined bodysuit, Hermione Sanchez tap-danced to "I'm a Yankee Doodle Dandy" as Jameson circled around the last row of folding chairs. By the time he made it beyond the far group of picnic tables, Vanessa had disappeared from his line of sight. He walked faster until he entered the marketplace area, after which he slowed a little to check out each booth as he passed it.

Where the hell had she wandered off to?

Not that it mattered. If it took him all afternoon, he would find her. He'd made up his mind to get a word with her, and he wouldn't give up until he got what he wanted.

Pie.

Van loved it. And she needed it. Jameson had started to get under her skin, the way he kept glancing over at her—the way she couldn't seem to make herself stop glancing back. He was a blue-eyed devil and her hopelessly hungry libido required a serious distraction from the temptation he posed.

If you asked Van, no finer distraction existed in the material world than pie.

She followed her nose to the booth where the Bronco Ladies Auxiliary sold just about every sort of baked treat known to man. One of the Abernathy ladies, Angela, gave her a tiny sample slice of cherry pie to help her choose between it and the apple raspberry.

Van got right to work on that sample, groaning aloud at the sweet, tangy taste and the perfectly flaky crust. "So good…"

"One of those Dalton boys baked it," said Angela with a big grin. "He brought us six of them.

We cut one up for samples, and four have sold already. We've only got one left."

"I want it."

"Twelve dollars," Angela smiled at her tauntingly.

"A bargain at the price."

Angela beamed. "Vanessa, it is yours." She started folding a pink bakery box as Van tried to make the sample last.

"Looks good," said the smooth, deep voice that haunted far too many of her dreams. It came from right behind her.

Carefully, she swallowed her bite of pie before slowly turning to face him. The sight of him so close kind of weakened her knees. In new jeans and a crisp black shirt, he looked yummier than her sliver of pie. "Jameson." Somehow, she kept her voice casual, friendly—but not *too* friendly. "How've you been?"

"Can't complain." He leaned in a little. She got a whiff of soap and leather, and she wanted to reach out and yank him in close just to smell him better. And then he smiled. "I didn't know you wore glasses."

Today, she wore the ones with the big tortoiseshell frames. Nervously, she adjusted them. "Sometimes it's just easier than contacts, you know? Not to mention more comfortable."

"I get that. You look good in them."

Too bad she felt so awkward and so completely unprepared to deal with him. "Thank you."

He nodded. "I'm thinking you look good in whatever you wear." He was still smiling.

And she couldn't stop herself from smiling right back—a real smile this time. He had that look in his eye, that teasing, tempting look she remembered with such pleasure from TNTNH, like she was the prettiest girl he'd ever seen and he couldn't take his eyes off her.

"You've got a dab of cherry filling," he said low, for her ears alone. And then, right there in front of God and everyone, he lifted a lean, tanned hand dusted with gleaming gold hairs and rubbed his thumb at the corner of her lower lip. Tingles shivered along every nerve ending she possessed.

Oh, she really shouldn't have let him do that.

And it got worse. He brought that thumb to his beautiful mouth and gave it a lick. Something low in her belly went liquid. Was Angela Abernathy watching?

Somehow, at this point, Van couldn't bring herself to care.

She stared at his mouth, admiring his close-trimmed dark gold beard and mustache—a Vandyke, they called it. Like Custer at the Little Big Horn, like David Beckham and Viggo Mortensen.

A Vandyke only looked good on a certain type of man.

The rugged, confident type.

"There's a pie contest on the Fourth," he said in a low, lazy drawl.

"I remember the pie contest." She dropped her used paper plate and plastic fork into the trash basket by the pie table. "It's held right here in Bronco Park at the town barbecue, am I right?" She might not live here anymore, but she knew her Red, White and Bronco events as well as any Bronco native. She sent a glance over her shoulder at Angela, just to see if the older woman had her eye on them. She didn't. Angela had already packed up Van's pie and moved on to filling a box with cookies for a good-looking fortyish woman Van didn't recognize.

"Are you planning on baking a pie to enter in the contest?" asked Jameson.

She faced him again. Had he moved in even closer—or was that merely wishful thinking on her part? "I don't bake, but I promise you, I will be eating."

He gave her a slow once-over, sending more tingles spreading through her traitorous body. Some men made her uncomfortable when they looked her up and down. Not Jameson. He just made her yearn.

"A girl who likes her pie," he said quietly.

"I'll take that is a compliment."

"Good. It was meant as one."

"As I recall, Miss Bronco always judges the pie contest," she said. At his nod, she added, "I'm betting on Charity to take the crown. She's talented and so pretty—and she has a way with words, too."

His eyes gleamed with pride as he said mildly, "I think she's doing well. And she's got her heart set on it, that's for sure."

"Tell her we're all rooting for her."

"That I will…" His voice wandered off into silence. He stared at her, and she stared back. Nobody else existed right then. She knew she should break the sudden spell that mutual attraction and scorching-hot memories had conjured between them.

But it just felt so good, standing there in dappled sunlight, the smell of pie on the air, staring at this beautiful man and almost wishing—

"Here you go, Vanessa." Angela Abernathy cut off Van's dangerous thoughts. She held out a pink bakery box. The cherry pie sat inside it. "How's it look?"

"Too delicious for words."

Angela tucked in the lid. "That's twelve dollars even."

Van traded her the money for the box. "Thanks."

"You are so welcome, dear."

"Hey, aren't you Vanessa Cruise, the one who teaches the summer camp kids out at Daphne Taylor's animal sanctuary?" The good-looking fortyish woman Van had noticed talking to Angela a moment ago moved closer just as Angela stepped away to wait on another customer. The woman had another pink bakery box in her hands.

"I'm Vanessa, yes."

"Lurline DuBois." The woman shifted the bakery box to her left hand and offered her right. Van gave it a shake. "I'm just off my second divorce and ready for a fresh start, if you take my meaning." Lurline slanted a smirk at Jameson. "How 'bout you, handsome? Got a name?"

Van introduced them. "Lurline, this is Jameson John."

Jameson, looking wary now, accepted the woman's hand and let go of it quickly. Lurline gave a loud laugh. "My, my. They do grow you boys up tall and strong here in Montana."

Was she making a move on Jameson?

For a moment, it looked that way—but then she surprised Van and turned to her again. "I heard about your students, how they got the Miss Bronco rules changed."

"Yes, they did." Van spoke with pride.

"I love that. I mean, why are beauty queens always barely more than babies? A real woman ought to toss her hat in the ring, show 'em how it should be done. I'm thinking next summer, I might just enter the contest myself." Lurline's eyes twinkled as she tossed her crow-black hair. "That is, if I'm still single."

"Go for it, Lurline." Van patted her shoulder—and remembered that cowboy in the purple shirt. He just might have a coronary if Lurline entered next year. So be it. Van's Young Adventurers hadn't fought for change so that everything could stay the same.

"Catch you two later." With a flirty smile and a jaunty wave, Lurline moved along, leaving the two of them staring after her.

"Lurline's a pistol," Jameson remarked wryly.

Van met his gaze. They both started laughing.

When the mirth faded to silence and they were left gazing too long into each other's eyes, he took her arm. She allowed him to pull her out of the Ladies Auxiliary booth, and into a space between that booth and the next one.

Carefully, she eased her arm free of his hold. "I should go."

"Wait." He had such gorgeous eyes, so clear, so vivid. So impossibly blue. Those eyes held her captive to memories she shouldn't allow herself—memories of his rough palm skating down her bare back, of his breath in her ear, his mouth doing incredible things to all her most secret places... "Just a phone number, Vanessa. That's all I'm asking for."

Her throat felt tight. She forced the words through it anyway. "It's a bad idea."

"No. It's a good idea. The *best* idea. I missed you. I can't stop thinking about you. Tell me to my face right now that since that night, you've never thought of me, never wondered what I might be doing, never considered looking me up. Just tell me you'd forgotten all about me. Just say it right to my face."

"I never thought of you." It came out flat, completely unconvincing.

He shook his head slowly. "Lying's beneath you."

She felt breathless and so sad, both at the same time. "We had an agreement."

He said nothing for an endless count of five. "Why? That's what I want to know. Why is it necessary that we can't get some coffee or maybe get dinner somewhere quiet, you and me?"

"It's a long story, one I don't care to share."

He glared at her. "I'm not giving up." And then, without another word, he turned on his boot heel and walked away.

She almost ran after him, to argue with him, insist at least one more time that TNTNH was never going to happen again.

Somehow, she kept her feet rooted in place.

Clutching her pie, she drew slow, even breaths as she counted to a hundred at a measured pace. Only after her pulse had settled down a little and her stomach felt at least marginally less fluttery did she head back to rejoin her family.

An hour after Van got back to her table, the Miss Bronco competition came to an end and the voting began.

Volunteers passed out the ballots, along with short pencils for anyone who needed one. Van voted for Charity and felt sure that just about everyone else in the park had, too. Jameson's sister stood out among the ten pretty young contestants, most of whom, as happened every year, were daughters of the influential families in town. Charity had that special something every beauty queen required. Not only was she gorgeous, she had a megawatt smile and a good head on her shoulders, and she came across as kind and thoughtful, too.

The volunteers moved through the crowd again, gathering the ballots and then disappearing into a tent set up specially for the purpose of tallying the votes.

As they waited for the results, Van got out the paper plates and plastic forks she'd bought on her way back to the table. Carefully, she took her pie from the pink box and proudly held it up for everyone to admire. "Who wants cherry pie? Baked by one of the Dalton boys and it is amazing."

Evan wanted a slice, and Callie had one, too.

Daphne, a strict vegetarian, voiced her suspicion that the Dalton boy who'd baked that pie had used lard rather than vegetable shortening. "And lard is made from animal fat. I guess I'll have to pass," she concluded regretfully.

Van put on a sad face. "I feel so bad for you." And then she grinned. "But hey. More for me." Both she and Daphne laughed.

Surprisingly, Van's students all claimed they weren't hungry. She found that a bit odd. Her students were *always* hungry.

And yet, the girls turned down the amazing pie and huddled together on the blanket, whispering to each other. Vanessa wondered vaguely what they might be up to. They giggled and nudged each other and whispered some more.

Whatever secrets they kept snickering over, they seemed to be having a terrific time. Well, more power to them, Vanessa thought as she cut an extra-large, mouthwatering slice for herself. Grabbing a plastic fork, she swung her legs to the other side of the bench.

With her back to the table, she could see the stage better, even if that position made it all too easy to let her gaze stray toward the John family table across the way. Uh-uh. Not going to happen. She kept her eyes trained on the stage.

The volunteers emerged from the tent. One carried an envelope up to the stage and passed it to Earl Tillson, who passed it to the mayor as another volunteer wheeled out a stand bearing two crowns on blue velvet pillows, one larger and more ornate than the other.

Earl called all ten contestants out from behind the curtain at the back of the stage. Last year's winner, an Abernathy cousin, stood at the mayor's side holding an enormous bouquet of red roses. The contestants lined up in their evening gowns wearing big smiles, their heads high and their shoulders back.

The mayor announced that Hermione Sanchez had taken fifth place. Her smile all the wider, Hermione stepped forward. To enthusiastic applause, last year's Miss Bronco handed her a single rose as Earl helped her into her green satin fifth-place sash. Fourth place went to one of the Taylors and third to another Abernathy. Van couldn't help thinking that the new rules hadn't changed much of anything, after all. Girls from Bronco's prominent families seemed to be winning, same as before.

However, she reminded herself, change didn't happen overnight. She remembered Lurline Du-Bois and grinned. Next year, the rules her Young

Adventurers had pushed for might inspire a whole new group of girls and women to compete.

The mayor announced, "And now we come to the first runner-up. Second only to Miss Bronco herself, the first runner-up is ever at the ready to assist Miss Bronco whenever she's called to help—and even to step in for Miss Bronco should scheduling conflicts occur. This year, our first runner-up is once again Miss Charity John!"

A slight silence elapsed before everyone started clapping. In that silence, Van felt sure she hadn't heard right. None of the others had compared to Charity. Of course she should have taken the crown.

But no. Van stared in disbelief as Charity, her beautiful smile a little bit wobbly, stepped forward to accept her single rose, the runner-up sash and the smaller of the two crowns.

"What's going on?" whispered a woman at the next table.

"Not a clue," replied another as murmurs of confusion and disapproval rose from the crowd.

Clearly, most everyone thought that Charity should have the big crown.

With a heavy sigh, Van forked up a giant bite of delicious pie. Sometimes the right person lost, but at least there was pie to ease the pain of life's disappointments.

She stuck that hunk of sweet, tart, saucy cherries and perfect, flaky crust into her mouth just as the mayor announced, "And this year's Miss Bronco, on a first-time ever write-in triumph, is Miss Vanessa Cruise!"

A gasp went up from half the spectators. Van choked on her pie so hard she sprayed cherries and crust all over her ripped jeans and soft, well-worn T-shirt.

This could not be happening.

Oh, but it was. "Get on up here, Vanessa!" shouted the mayor. "Join us on the stage and claim your crown!"

Chapter Three

As Van brushed bits of crust and cherry filling off her jeans, her Young Adventurer girls jumped up to surround her. Like a flock of birds at a feeding station, they all twittered at once as they clapped and high-fived each other.

Cleo Davidson, wearing a wide, proud smile, grabbed Van's hand and pulled her upright. "Come on! You need to get up there. They're waiting for you."

"Yes!" crowed eleven-year-old Emma Bledsoe. "We did it! We got you written in. You won, Miss Cruise. You will be the best Miss Bronco ever!" She and Cleo high-fived each other yet again.

"Girl power!" shouted twelve-year-old Mandy Highwalker and held up her hand.

"Girl power!" the others hollered in unison, each reaching up to slap Mandy's palm, one after the other.

Loudly congratulating each other, they herded Van toward the stage. A frantic glance back at the table revealed Evan, Daphne and Callie, staring after her, looking bemused.

Van mouthed, "Help!" at her roomie and Callie gave her a determined smile and a big thumbs-up—whatever that meant.

Numbly, she mounted the side steps leading up the stage.

Last year's Miss Bronco came to meet her halfway. "Congratulations, Vanessa," the girl said in a sweet and silky voice. Gently, she took Van's hand. "This way…" And she led Van to center stage.

Dumbfounded, Van tried to pull herself together, but she felt pretty much immobilized at what had just happened. She ended up staring blankly out at the crowd, registering random facial expressions—everything from glee to fury to total bewilderment.

The former Miss Bronco handed her the winner's massive armful of roses and then helped her juggle them in order to settle the victory sash across Van's cherry-stained Science Is Like Magic—but Real T-shirt.

Carefully, after last year's winner set the crown on her head, Van reached up and straightened her glasses. As she did that, her gaze slid to the John family's table, where Jameson looked troubled. He probably didn't know how to feel about his beautiful, talented sister losing to his one-night stand from New Year's Eve.

His mother looked crushed, and his father shouted angrily, "What's the damn point, I ask you? This is ridiculous. We don't need a Miss Bronco who didn't even bother to compete. How can this be happening when several talented young ladies gave their all for the crown today? And come on, just look at her. Old jeans and a baggy shirt? Look at the expression on her face. She doesn't even want to be up there!"

Vanessa's head spun and her stomach roiled. She drowned in a sea of conflicting emotions. She felt pride at what Cleo, Emma, Mandy and the rest of the girls had accomplished. Yet at the same time, she couldn't help mostly agreeing with Jameson's dad. The write-in rule sucked. Why hadn't she realized that earlier and convinced her Young Adventurers that it had to go?

It wasn't fair. She hadn't competed. She'd never *wanted* to compete. And now she wore the crown that Charity John truly deserved.

Random voices called out, demanding a recount.

Earl tried to shout them down, but they wouldn't be silenced until the volunteers counted every ballot for a second time right there on the stage. As they retallied every vote, Van, the ten actual contestants, the mayor, Earl and the former Miss Bronco stood up there and waited.

That process seemed to last forever and a day. Vanessa spent most of the recount clutching her roses while secretly rooting for the agonizing process to end her unexpected reign before it could really begin.

She did not get her wish. Somehow, her Young Adventurers had convinced a clear majority of voters to write in her name—all without anyone telling Van what they were up to.

When the mayor declared Van the winner—again—most of the crowd applauded with enthusiasm, after which the mayor invited her to say a few words.

A speech? He had to be kidding her.

But he wasn't.

She pulled it together, praising the skill and heart of the ten real contestants and thanking the people of Bronco, especially her brilliant, resourceful Young Adventurers. Almost all the spectators actually applauded when she finished, so she supposed her impromptu acceptance speech hadn't been *that* bad.

At last, Earl Tillson took over again. He thanked everyone for coming and reminded them to get their tickets for the rodeo tomorrow and not to miss the big barbecue on Independence Day or the Favorite Pet Contest July fifth out at Happy Hearts Animal Sanctuary.

He added with enthusiasm, "As all of you are probably aware, our lovely Miss Bronco will be hosting all three events. Be sure to attend, folks. Red, White and Bronco is an important and meaningful town tradition, one none of us can afford to miss."

A last burst of applause followed and finally, the crowd began to disperse.

Van remembered her manners and thanked Earl, the previous Miss Bronco and the other contestants. Before she could make her escape, a woman slipped out from between the curtains at the rear of the stage, marched straight to Van and introduced herself as Maureen Kelly, pageant coordinator. She took Van's email address and phone number so that she could get in touch with her when necessary.

Maureen promised, "As soon as I finish up here, I'll email you the list of events at which you'll be expected to appear. The list includes your duties at each event, what time you'll need to be there and with whom you should check in when you arrive."

Though Van longed to rip off her crown, tear the victory sash from her chest, toss the roses over her shoulder and sprint away screaming, she answered politely, "Thank you so much, Maureen."

When Van finally escaped the stage, Callie, Evan, Daphne and the still-excited Young Adventurers met Van at the foot of the steps. They surrounded her with hugs and congratulations. Evan suggested pizza for all, his treat. Not all the girls could come, but the ringleaders' parents gave permission. They went to Bronco Brick Oven Pizza and claimed a big table.

The girls were still flying high with the success of their campaign to transform the Miss Bronco beauty pageant. They kept offering toasts, raising their draft root beers high. Van tried to keep a positive attitude in order not to bring her day campers down.

She waited until she and Callie got home alone to let her true feelings show.

"This is awful," she moaned, bracing her elbows on the kitchen table and burying her face in her hands.

Callie scooted her chair closer, wrapped an arm around Van's shoulders and gave her a side hug. "It will be fine," she soothed.

"Fine? There are *events*," Van cried. "Starting tomorrow with the big rodeo out at the fairgrounds. I'm supposed to greet people and make introductions and walk around the arena smiling till my face breaks, doing the fancy pageant wave." She pulled out her phone and checked her email, opening the big file from the pageant director. "Fifty pages here on where I need to be—*appropriately* dressed, wearing my sash and crown or a flashy hat—for every event I'll be hosting and/or attending within the next year. I'm even cutting the ribbon at the end of the month when they open the remodeled convention center. They want me to give a speech for that, to talk about change and growth and the power of working together in our community."

Callie side hugged her a little tighter. "How about if you just breathe deep and take it one step at a time?"

"One step? But there are so many steps. How am I going to be Miss Bronco all year from Billings? Not to mention, being a beauty queen is completely not me. I just keep thinking I need to resign and let Charity take the crown. No one can argue that she wants and deserves to win."

Callie rubbed Van's back and asked gently, "You really think you can do that to your girls at Young Adventurers?"

Van groaned. "Oh God, no. But why didn't they warn me? Why didn't they at least give me a chance to explain all the reasons that writing me in was a bad, bad idea?"

"Well, because they wanted you to win and they weren't taking any chances you might say no, that's why. But you're right that they shouldn't have added the write-in rule. It's not fair that someone who didn't even enter can beat out contestants who got up there and gave their all for a chance to win."

"Exactly."

"The good news is I'm betting we can find a way to change that rule for next year."

"Next year? What about right now? I'm not beauty queen material. Never have been, never *wanted* to be."

"Van. You're beautiful and smart and not the least bit shy. You're a teacher. You know how to get up in front of people and make yourself heard."

"It's not the same."

"Yeah, it kind of is. You're just not giving yourself enough credit."

"Oh, trust me. When it comes to the beauty queen thing, I don't *want* any credit. It's not who I—" A knock at the door cut her off before she could really get her rant on. "What now? Are we expecting someone?"

With a shrug, Callie pushed back her chair and went down the entry hallway to the door. She must have peered through the peephole. A moment later, she darted back into sight. "It's

Charity," she whispered. "And her hot brother Jameson is with her."

Jameson. Van's silly heart pounded too fast. She did not need more time around her annoyingly unforgettable one-night stand. As for Charity, Van wouldn't mind a word or two with Jameson's sister. She could smooth things over, at least, confess how crappy she felt about the way things had turned out today.

"Up to you," Callie said.

"Go ahead. Let them in."

"Good choice," Callie said with a nod. She turned and disappeared down the hall again. Van heard her open the door. "Charity." Callie's voice was warm, welcoming. "Jameson. Hello. Come on in, you two."

Van jumped to her feet as Charity and her brother emerged from the narrow hallway. "Hey."

Charity, so pretty and pulled together in dressy jeans and a lavender top, shifted the giant pink binder she carried to her right hand and took hold of Jameson's arm with her left. "I had to come. I had to see how you're doing." She glanced up at her big brother. "I dragged Jameson along for moral support."

Jameson patted his sister's hand and then removed his hat. "Happy to help any way I can."

Oh, I'll just bet you are. Van kept her expression calm as she met his gleaming blue eyes.

"How thoughtful of you." She kind of wanted to scream. But she didn't.

Callie gestured at the table. "Sit down, everyone. Please."

Charity sat on Van's left. Jameson hooked his hat on the back of the chair to Van's right and sat there. Callie took the last seat, the one across from Van.

Charity set her huge pink binder in front of her and gave it a little push toward the center of the table. Then she leaned closer to Van. "I just needed to see if you're all right. You looked so shocked today—I mean, you handled yourself really well, but still. I could see that you'd been taken completely by surprise."

Van looked in those blue eyes so much like Jameson's and felt humbled. "Wait. You're worried about *me*?"

Charity put her slim hand over Van's. "Of course. It's a big job being Miss Bronco, and it's not as if you applied for the position."

"I, well, you're right about that. And I..." Okay, so maybe Charity had an ulterior motive here. She'd come to suggest that Van step down, leaving Charity to accept the crown she should have had in the first place. Nothing wrong with that. In fact, it sounded like the perfect outcome for Van, too. "Okay, here's the deal. I had no idea that this would happen, and I can't help thinking my best move now is to step down and let you claim the crown you so completely deserve."

Across the table, Callie stiffened. Van knew her friend worried how the Young Adventurers would react to such a decision, but Callie also knew it wasn't her choice to make. She kept her mouth shut.

Too bad Charity didn't. "No! Vanessa, you can't."

Van blinked. "Huh? But I thought—"

Charity shook her head. Her thick, golden curls shifted and shimmered like a river of silk. "I mean it. You can't. True, it didn't go the way we expected it would. I was shocked, too. I really thought it was finally my year."

"Because you deserve to win."

"No." Charity sat up straighter. "That's just not so. A lot of people wrote your name on their ballots. You are the chosen Miss Bronco, and the truth is I'm just…not." She grabbed Vanessa's hand and stared deep in her eyes. "It's your job, your *duty* to rise to the occasion."

"But I don't even live here anymore."

"You're a Bronco girl and everyone knows it— and it's okay, Vanessa." She added, with feeling, "I promise you it's all going to work out. Because I'm going to help you—and I know, I know. Jameson mentioned that you live in Billings now. But really, Billings is not *that* far away."

"Jameson mentioned that, did he?" She slanted a dark glance at the maddeningly hot man on her other side. In return, he gave her a slow, knowing smile. Across the table, Callie watched them much too closely.

Charity demanded, "Did you get your schedule from Maureen?"

Confused, Van turned to Charity again. "Uh, Maureen?"

"The pageant coordinator."

"Oh. Yes. I did." She tried not to scowl. "All fifty pages of it."

"Have you had a chance to look it over yet?"

"Well, I…"

"When you do, you'll notice that the Miss Bronco events after summertime are few and far between. It's all going to be workable. You'll see. I know what I'm talking about. I've been doing this every year since I was sixteen. And I'm going to teach you everything you need to know."

Wait! No! she wanted to shout.

But she knew she couldn't. Charity was right, damn it. And the pretty blonde's passion and enthusiasm for the tradition of Miss Bronco made Van want to grab her in a great big hug—so she did.

Charity hugged her right back.

And then Callie broke out the snacks and cold drinks. Charity opened her giant pink binder, which turned out to be her own personal planner, a blueprint for Miss Bronco success.

For the next two hours, the four of them munched Cheez-Its and trail mix as Charity guided Van through everything from what to wear for her upcoming appearances to the main points she should hit when speaking at various gatherings. Van kept her focus on the job at hand—mostly.

Yet she couldn't forget who sat on her other side. More than once, she got distracted by his low, sexy chuckle. She would shoot him a furtive glance and then have trouble looking away again. When Charity asked for her phone number, she gave it and then couldn't stop herself from sliding another look at her top-secret lover from TNTNH. That steady gaze of his was as compelling as ever. And those lips she'd loved kissing way too much twitched at the corners with a hint of a grin. She knew his thoughts exactly—she'd insisted no numbers would ever be exchanged but he'd gotten her digits, after all.

"Come on." Charity took her hand. "Take me to your room. Let's decide what you're wearing tomorrow."

It felt weird, to leave Jameson and Callie alone. Callie had a look like she might go a little bit rogue and press for answers to questions Van didn't want her asking.

But Charity gave a tug and Van found herself up out of her chair, following Jameson's sister down the hall to the second bedroom. They weren't in there long. She showed Charity a pair of red jeans, her best boots and couple of dressy Western shirts she'd brought with her from Billings. Charity chose the blue one with the white trim and silver stitching, declaring that the silver thread would really pop with her rhinestone crown.

"Me, in a crown." Van shook her head, readjusted her glasses and grinned. "Never thought I'd see the day."

Charity beamed. "You're going to look fantastic. You need to be at the fairgrounds at 1:00 p.m., right? I'll be here at noon to do a final wardrobe and hair check, and then we'll ride to the fairgrounds together."

Tomorrow was Saturday. Weekends Daphne welcomed any and all Young Adventurers to Happy Hearts. Van didn't teach classes on weekends. But on Saturday, as a rule, she dropped by for morning coffee with Daphne and Evan, after which she would stay and help out if Daphne needed her.

"Noon works," she said. She could easily stop in at Happy Hearts, work for an hour or two at whatever chores needed doing, and still have time to pull herself together for her "wardrobe check."

As she led Charity back to the main room, she could hear Callie talking about her job with Evan at Bronco Ghost Tours. "He's a taskmaster, Van's brother. But in a good way. I like the work. Never a dull moment when ghosts are involved." Callie laughed. "And did you hear? Van and Evan's great-grandmother, Winona, has opened a shop right there with us on the premises. She's billing herself as sort of a cross been a life coach and a psychic. If you need guidance or advice, Winona can help."

"You're telling me that *the* Winona Cobbs has a psychic shop at Bronco Ghost Tours?"

"Essentially, yes," Callie replied, as Van and Charity rejoined them at the table. "She moved to Bronco from up in Rust Creek Falls after meeting Van and her family down here. Did you hear that it turned out Van's grandma Dorothea is Winona's long-lost daughter?"

"Wow," said Charity.

Jameson slid Van a knowing look. "I did hear that, yes."

"Anyway, Winona is very wise," Callie said. "She really does give great advice." She asked Jameson, "You've heard of 'Wisdom by Winona'?"

"Of course. That column was syndicated. I was a fan back in the day."

"You should come by, check it out."

"I just might." He looked straight at Van then,

a lazy sort of look, intimate and smoldering. "Never hurts to get some good advice about all the important things. Money. Love. Whether or not all my secret dreams will ever come true…"

Charity, completely oblivious to her brother's real agenda, picked up her pink binder and chirped brightly, "Okay, then. Tomorrow. Right here at noon."

"I'll be here," Van promised.

Charity aimed her dazzling smile at her brother. "Jameson, you ready?"

"You bet." He unfolded his long, strong frame from the kitchen chair, grabbed his hat and followed his sister to the door. "Nice to see you, Callie," he said as they went out. "Vanessa." He gave her another one of those scorching-hot looks. Her hormones cried out at all the months of unfulfilled longing. "It's been a pleasure."

She pasted on a smile, muttered, "'Bye, now," and quickly shut the door.

The next morning, Van found Daphne alone at the kitchen table in the Happy Hearts farmhouse, her sweet yellow Lab, Barkley, snoozing at her feet.

"Where's Evan?" Van headed straight for the coffee maker. Though Daphne usually drank tea, she had coffee ready for anyone who wanted it.

Daphne worked a bit of hay out of her haphazard ponytail. She always rose before the crack of dawn and went out to look after the animals first. Tea and breakfast came later. "Winona summoned him. She needed some help moving things around out at her shop. It seems the spirits have their own specific requirements concerning what has to go where."

"Feng shui matters, in this world or the next."

Daphne nodded. "Apparently so."

Van smiled at the idea of her often-gruff big brother rushing to do Winona's bidding. "He can be such a tough guy, that fiancé of yours, but he's good to his great-grandma."

"Yes, he is. Hungry?"

"I ate with Callie, thanks." Van took her usual chair at the table. Barkley got up, came over for a scratch behind the ear and then settled back down next to Daphne. "So what's going on at Happy Hearts today?"

"You know, I'm almost afraid to say it out loud, but we're actually pretty much on top of things— for the moment, anyway. As we speak, there are ten young, hardworking volunteers outside mucking stalls, feeding the goats and cleaning out the cat barn." Yep. Happy Hearts had a whole barn where the cats and kittens lived.

Van felt relieved. "Glad to hear everything's under control. I can't stay that long today. I have to head back to Callie's by ten thirty or so to get ready for the rodeo this afternoon."

"That's right." Daphne set down her mug. "Miss Bronco will be making an appearance."

"Oh yes, she will—and is it weird that we're talking about her in the third person?"

Daphne snickered, "You mean, given that she's you?"

"Exactly. Who knew *that* would happen? Oh, guess who came to see me yesterday evening."

"Not a clue."

"Charity John." Van brought her future sister-in-law up to speed on her visit from Charity and Jameson, taking care to mention Jameson only as an afterthought, keeping the focus strictly on Charity's kindness and generosity. "I really like her," Van added. "She's not only a truly good person who's willing to help me get Miss Bronco right, but she's also given me a whole new appreciation for the, er, Miss Bronco tradition."

"More people should be like Charity." Daphne frowned into her empty mug. When she glanced up again, Van saw shadows in her blue eyes. Daphne had something weighing on her mind. "I think I need one more cup," she said. "You?"

"Please." Van waited until Daphne had fixed herself more tea and refilled Van's mug to ask, "What is it? What's wrong?"

Daphne puffed out her cheeks with a heavy

breath. "I wish more people were like Charity John. But they're not. Some get so set in their ways they can't accept any kind of change at all. And some are just so entitled. Yesterday, when you won the crown, there was some grumbling about how you hadn't even entered, and you didn't deserve to be Miss Bronco."

"I heard some of that. Randall John shouted it right out." She shrugged. "You have to admit, he kind of has a point."

Daphne gave her a sideways look. "So you're not upset about that stuff?"

"No, I'm not. I *didn't* enter. It's completely logical that some people would be pissed off about that. For a half second or so, I even considered stepping down."

Daphne gasped. "What? No! Don't do that."

"Don't worry, I'm not. All the Bronco old guard will have to get over themselves. I've got Charity on my side, and all my Young Adventurers are looking to me to stand up and be counted for fairness and change."

"Excellent. That's what I needed to hear." Somehow, as Daphne spoke, she visibly deflated until, once again, she stared down into her fresh cup of tea. "I do love your attitude. I love it a lot." She sounded downright sad.

Van reached over and squeezed Daphne's arm. "What has gotten you down?"

"You don't need to hear it." Daphne stared into the cup some more, her expression glum.

"If you need to say it, I need to hear it. This isn't really about the pageant, is it?"

Daphne glanced up. She wrinkled her pretty nose. "It's just my dad. It never ends with him."

"Wait a minute. Your dad? I thought everything had worked out between you and him."

Daphne pushed her cup away. "Not exactly..." Cornelius Taylor did not in any way approve of her vegetarianism *or* that she'd created Happy Hearts, where, her father claimed, she made "pets out of livestock."

"Daphne, are you trying to tell me that you and your dad didn't reconcile, after all?"

"Back at Christmas, I felt we were doing better with each other, kind of easing our way onto the same page. But the good feelings didn't last. He just doesn't approve of me and it shows. Things have really been going downhill between us again lately."

"What happened, exactly?"

"Well, for instance, last night, after the pageant, Evan and I went out to the ranch for a family barbecue. My dad got all over me for not eating the ribs and started in about what a laughingstock I've made of him with Happy Hearts."

Van wrapped a comforting arm across Daphne's

shoulders. "That's just wrong. What is the matter with him?"

"I don't know. The down stroke is we're right back where we started, as far as I'm concerned. I'm not giving up Happy Hearts, and I'm never eating animal flesh."

"Of course you're not."

"Yeah, well, my dad just refuses to accept that. At this point, I'm not even sure he's going to come to our wedding." She and Evan were getting married in October.

Van took Daphne's hand and wrapped both of hers around it. "Hey. He's your dad and he loves you. One way or another, he's going to be there to walk you down the aisle."

Daphne's smile didn't reach her eyes. "That's pretty much what Evan said."

"Because it's true."

"Yeah, it's true to you and Evan because of how you grew up. Things were different for me."

"What are you talking about? We had problems with our father, too. Big ones. Our dad deserted us. He walked out and never looked back." He'd also taken every cent the family owned right along with him.

"It was awful, what your dad did. But I'm not talking about him. I'm talking about your mom and your grandmother. They would walk through fire for you. And now you have Winona, and she is amazing, too. On the other hand, my mother's remarried."

"And lives in Billings, right?"

"That's right. I hardly see her anymore. My first stepmother is long gone. As for my current stepmother, well, at least Jessica tries. We get along well enough, though I wouldn't say we're close. I love my brothers, but they can be as bull-headed as my dad. Sometimes I feel like a cuckoo hatched in a nest of eagles."

Van couldn't bear the pain on Daphne's face. "No. Uh-uh. Come here." She reached out again. Daphne kind of fell toward her. They hugged between their chairs. Down on the floor, Barkley whined at them in doggy sympathy.

As Van rubbed Daphne's back and whispered words of comfort and understanding, she found herself thinking how right Daphne was about Van's family. Life hadn't always been easy in the small house on West Street where her mom had been forced to move after her dad ran off with all their savings. Yet somehow, they'd scraped by. Never once in all the years in that little house had Van lacked for love or understanding.

Too bad her mom and Grandma Daisy disagreed with her decision to make her life in Billings. They both wanted her to find happiness in Bronco. As for Great-Grandmother Winona, she'd made it more than clear that she agreed with them.

Well, too bad. Not going to happen. Nine years ago, when Van left for college with her heart shattered and her pride in tatters, she'd made herself a promise never to move back. She'd had enough of her hometown, of mean girls who mocked her, of the boy who'd once said he would love her forever—and then made her into an object of ridicule, hatred and derision at Bronco High. She would return to visit the people she loved, but never to stay.

Then again, though her mom and grandmother—and now, her newly found great-grandmother, too—disagreed with her choices, they loved her unconditionally anyway. They would never treat her callously, the way Cornelius did Daphne. As she held Daphne and whispered reassurances that everything would work out with her dad in the end, Van felt gratitude welling toward the two strong women who had raised her, the grandfather she missed every day and the big brother who could be gruff and bossy but always had her back.

And toward Winona, with her generous heart, her ingrained kindness, and the weird and wonderful wisdom she was only too eager to share with everyone she met.

A half an hour later, as Van drove back to the apartment, she tried really hard not to wonder if Jameson would show up with Charity. "He'd better not," she muttered under her breath to no one in particular. Scowling out the windshield at the bright, sunny day, she staunchly ignored the anticipation in her heart and the silly, fluttery sensation in her belly.

Chapter Four

Charity, looking gorgeous in dark-wash jeans and a blue shirt with rhinestones glittering on the collar, arrived at Callie's right on time. She'd pinned her blond hair into a perfectly tousled updo, carried a small suitcase under her arm—and had Jameson in tow.

"Gotta support my little sis." Faking an innocent expression, he looked right at Van.

Charity patted his sculpted jaw with its perfectly trimmed short beard. "You are my favorite big brother."

He grinned down at her. "I've heard you say the same thing to both Dawson and Maddox."

Charity let out a peal of happy laughter.

"Busted." She turned to Van and Callie. "I got super lucky in the big-brother department. Now let's get to work. Callie and Jameson, make yourselves comfortable out here. Vanessa, lead me to your makeup area."

Van had her own bathroom right next to her bedroom. She took Charity in there. The dinky counter had just enough space for Charity's small suitcase, which turned out to be a professional makeup kit, the kind that opened out, accordion-style, into tiers. The kit contained over a hundred different eye shadow choices, a wide array of makeup brushes and foundation colors to match any skin tone.

Once Charity had her kit arranged to her liking, she whipped out a white cloth and draped it over Van's shirt. "Don't look so horrified. This isn't a makeover."

Van glanced heavenward. "Thank you, Lord, for small favors."

"As your personal Miss Bronco coach, I'm all about you doing you, Vanessa."

"And I like that. A lot."

"I'm only going to enhance your natural beauty." Charity frowned and accused, "You've covered your freckles—or most of them, anyway."

"Sometimes I like them, and sometimes they annoy me."

"And this is one of those days when you're annoyed with them?"

"Pretty much, yeah."

Charity peered closer. "Are you wearing contacts?"

"I am." Van pointed her thumb at her chest. "Beauty queen here—not that I don't love my glasses. I do. But they're one accessory too many once I add my crown."

"Yes, I think you're right." Humming under her breath, Charity went to work with her fancy brushes and endless pots of blush, lip color and eye shadow. Not ten minutes later, she took a step back. "There. Perfect."

Van peered at her reflection. She didn't look made up, but her eyes appeared larger and her skin had a new glow. "It's great."

"And so simple." Charity ran down a quick makeup tutorial tailored to Van's coloring, skin type and the shape of her face. She insisted that Van keep the brushes and makeup she'd used. "Tomorrow, you can do it yourself. I'll stop by again before the big barbecue just to give you my seal of approval."

"Charity, you're a wonder."

Charity's glowing smile shone all the brighter. "Why, thank you, Vanessa." Next, she primped Van's hair. "Where's your crown and sash?"

Van gave her a slow look from under her eyelashes. "You know, the more I think about it, the more I think I'll just pass on those today."

Charity wasn't having that. "We both know you can't do that—well, maybe you can skip the crown. That's more for formal occasions. And as it happens, I brought over a few pretty hats just in case. You can wear one of them."

"Do you always come prepared for any eventuality?"

"I try." Charity put on a stern expression. "But you're wearing your sash. Don't try to get out of it."

Van fluttered her eyelashes. "I wouldn't dream of it."

Jameson whistled in appreciation when Charity led Van back out to the main room. "Miss Bronco," he said, "you're even more beautiful than before."

Was he wearing her down with the hot looks, the flattery and the teasing?

Well, maybe a little. He was always so charming, the very definition of irresistible. No matter how often she reminded herself that she needed distance from the man, a certain rebellious streak deep in her heart couldn't help looking forward to the next time she might see him.

She desperately wished she could actually forget The Night That Never Happened.

"Your sister knows her way around a makeup kit," Van said.

Charity seemed pleased. "A few enhancements never hurt. Now let's get going."

"Plenty of room in my truck," Jameson said. "We can all ride together."

Forbidden images of their night together dancing in her head, Van nipped his suggestion firmly in the bud. "Callie and I will follow you two."

Charity grabbed her hand. "First, we need to choose your hat." The four of them left the apartment and gathered around Jameson's big, black quad cab, from which Charity produced three gorgeous spangled hats. She tossed two of them back onto the rear seat and held up the third. It was snowy white with an actual tiara sewn on above the brim.

"This one," she declared. "It's a crown and a hat at the same time." She placed it at a jaunty angle on Van's head. "Perfect." Charity primped a couple of Van's loose, dark curls in a proprietary manner. Really, Van thought, Jameson's sister was a sheer delight. "You have your sash?" Charity demanded.

Nodding resignedly, Van held it up.

"All right, then," said Charity. "We're ready to go."

* * *

Jameson felt more than a little disappointed that Vanessa gave him zero chance to persuade her to ride with him. Instead, he had to watch her follow Callie past her silver Subaru to an olive-green Jeep. Vanessa took the passenger side and Callie slid in behind the wheel.

"Well?" asked his bossy little sister. "Are we standing here in the parking lot all day for some reason?"

He turned and chucked her under the chin. "Get in and let's go."

The Bronco fairgrounds consisted of a giant, open, graded field on rolling land not far outside town. Both Jameson and Callie found spots in the main parking lot, but he knew that by the end of the day, trucks and SUVs would fill the overflow lot farther out.

Jameson had planned ahead and bought plenty of tickets two weeks before, enough for his whole family and then some. He gave Vanessa and Callie two of the extras so none of them had to wait in line to get them. Once they were through the gate, Charity led Vanessa off to take care of Miss Bronco business. He and Callie climbed the stands to claim enough space for four in one of the rows of benches.

"There they are." Callie pointed into the arena, where Vanessa was shaking hands with a tall, powerfully built cowboy. Even from up on the stands, that cowboy looked a whole lot like the guy who played the lead role in the *Creed* movies. "That's Geoff Burris, isn't it?" Callie asked.

"The one and only." Burris, Bronco born and raised, was currently setting the rodeo circuit on fire. Women loved the guy. Jameson sat forward. He watched Vanessa closely for any sign that she found Geoff as fascinating as everyone else did. He relaxed a little when he saw her smile. It was friendly and easy, that smile—with none of the heat he felt when she looked at *him*. Now, if he could just get her to admit that their one night had not been anywhere close to enough...

Callie said, "I heard we might get the Mistletoe Rodeo right here in Bronco, at the convention center in November. I also heard that Geoff is a big part of why that might happen."

Jameson nodded, his eyes on the action down below. A couple of the clowns led out a white mare with a thick white mane and tail to match. They gave Van a boost into the saddle. "It never hurts," Jameson said, "when a homegrown cowboy grows up to be a rodeo champion. Hey, I didn't know Vanessa could ride."

Callie shrugged. "Looks that way to me."

Earl Tillson, apparently the official announcer for all the Red, White and Bronco events this year, introduced the new Miss Bronco. Waving and flashing her pearly whites, Vanessa rode the mare around the arena. God, she was gorgeous—and already coming into her own as a special kind of beauty queen, one with attitude and sass and her own personal style.

By then, the stands were full. The roar of applause, whistles and stomping feet filled the air. One or two yahoos booed. Jameson stiffened and started to rise.

Callie reached across the two spaces they were saving and grabbed his arm. "Easy, cowboy. Some people are still upset about Van's surprise win. Let them blow off a little steam."

Scowling, he stayed in his seat and muttered, "They kick up much more sand, I'm dealing with them."

"So…" Callie drew out the word. "What's really happening between you two?"

He grunted. "Me and Geoff Burris? Not a thing."

"Har-har. You and Van. She claims there's nothing, but she and I have gotten real close the last month or so. I can read her, and I see the way you look at her. There's something."

"No clue what you're talkin' about, Callie."

"You know you're fooling no one, right?"

He pretended not to hear that and kept his focus on Vanessa as she finished her circle of the arena and dismounted. One of the clowns led the mare away. His sister joined Vanessa. Charity had already spotted him and Callie. She said something to Vanessa, who nodded. They left the arena.

A few minutes later, they sidled their way along the row toward Jameson and Callie, Charity in the lead, which worked out great. Charity stepped past him and took the seat next to Callie, leaving an empty space with Charity on one side and Jameson on the other. He scooted close to his sister, which left Vanessa the empty space on his other side.

She sat. The rhinestones on her hat caught the afternoon sun and glittered. He wanted to grab her and kiss her.

Of course, he did no such thing. But he did lean her way until his arm brushed hers and the scent of her tempted him. "You looked great out there. Didn't know you could ride."

"You'd be surprised at the things I know."

"I have no doubt of that."

She met his eyes then, a hint of a smile curving those lush lips of hers. "It's true I grew up in a split-level on West Street. But back in my teens, I used to work summers out at the Ambling A, saving up for college and to earn spending money. I mucked stalls and fed pigs. That old guy, the cook, Malone?"

Everybody knew Malone. And Malone seemed to know everyone's secrets. "I know Malone."

"Well, Malone said it was a damn crime, a Bronco girl who didn't ride. He kind of made it his mission to teach me."

Charity bumped his arm. He frowned at her. "What?"

"Callie has to go."

Vanessa's roommate held up her phone. "Guys, sorry. Text from Evan. He needs me immediately to make a few emergency tweaks to the tour route for tonight."

"He *always* needs you immediately," Vanessa grumbled.

"What can I say? I'm indispensable." Callie was smiling. If Evan Cruise made her work too hard, at least she seemed to enjoy the job.

"I've made my appearance," said Vanessa. "I'll go with—"

"You can't!" Charity cut her off before Jameson could do it. "Miss Bronco never walks out on the Red, White and Bronco rodeo. We'll take you home—right, Jameson?"

He hid his satisfied smile. "Of course."

"Well, I—"

"Stay." Charity reached across Jameson to pat Vanessa's knee as Callie said goodbye and headed off down the row away from them.

Jameson leaned into his favorite brunette again. "Hungry?"

Of course, his sister answered before Vanessa could say a word. "Yes! I'm dying for a Coke. Get us both a pop and a hot dog, won't you, Jameson—and popcorn, too?"

He asked Vanessa, "That sound all right to you?"

She looked at him, her gaze straying to his mouth, then snapping back up again. "Thank you."

"Anytime." He would fetch and carry a thousand hot dogs, bring her kegs full of pop just to get her to look at him the way she was right now—like she couldn't help wanting to kiss him again.

She fished some bills from a pocket and held them out.

He slowly shook his head.

"I like to pay my own way," she said.

"I've got it, no problem." He held her dark gaze, thinking how good it felt every time he stared into her big brown eyes.

Finally, she gave in and stuck the bills back in her pocket.

Only then did he rise. "'Scuse me." She slanted her knees to the side, and he headed off toward the nearest concession booth.

It took a while. When he returned, Vanessa and

Charity were whispering together, leaning over the empty seat they'd saved for him. As soon as he reached them, Vanessa scooted closer to Charity, as though his little sister might save her from his bad self.

Hiding a grin, he dropped down beside her and passed out the treats. On the dirt down below, bareback riding and steer wrestling had come and gone. And just after Earl Tillson announced team roping, some smart-ass a few rows back spoke too loudly for his own damn good. "Hey, look. That's the fake Miss Bronco right there."

"Yeah," said some other fool, as Jameson slid his hot dog and root beer under his seat. "Where does she get off, stealing the crown like she thinks she's got a right?"

Charity, Coke in one hand, hot dog in the other, started to stand to confront them.

Jameson reached behind Vanessa to clasp her shoulder. "I'll take care of them," he said quietly. "Be right back."

"Wait—" Vanessa tried to stop him. Too bad she had both hands full.

And he was already on his feet, mounting the benches, striding straight up between seated spectators, scattering "'Scuse mes" as he went.

The two troublemakers, both of whom Jameson recognized as local kids a year or two younger than

Charity, snickered as he reached their row. One of them sneered, "What's your problem, man?"

"Gentlemen," Jameson replied in an even tone. "The way I see it, we have two options at this point. You apologize to the rightfully chosen Miss Bronco here and now. Or you and me head on out to the parking lot where we can avoid blocking anyone's view of the hardworking cowboys down in the dirt and discuss this unfortunate situation at length." By then, both troublemakers were looking a tad worried.

"Apologize, you fools," growled a middle-aged man down the row.

The skinnier of the two kids sent a glare at the older man and jumped to his feet. Sticking out his scrawny chest, he blustered, "Bring it!"

The other kid frowned, but he did get up.

Jameson led them out to the aisle and down to the ground. He was halfway to one of the side exits when he heard frantic whispering behind him. Counting silently to himself, he kept walking.

Five seconds elapsed before he heard two sets of boots take off at a run. Jameson turned to watch them flee—through the nearby exit and into the parking lot. He considered giving chase but figured the two had embarrassed themselves enough for one day. He headed back up into the stands again.

"Everything okay?" Charity asked when he sat down.

"Just fine. I think those two boys must've left the gas on at home. They ran off before we had a chance to communicate."

Charity chuckled. "I remember them from high school. All hat, no cattle."

Down below, a roper flanked and tied—smooth, clean and fast. The stands erupted in applause, the two troublemaking young fools long forgotten.

By everyone but Vanessa. She leaned close. "I am a schoolteacher, you know. I could've handled those two kids."

That gave him another perfect opportunity to look into those deep, dark eyes again. "I know you could. But I see no reason why you have to fight every battle all on your own."

The next hour and a half passed too quickly. To no one's surprise, Geoff Burris triumphed, taking home a fine purse and the coveted Red, White and Bronco belt buckle. As they got up to go, Jameson had his mind on how to somehow get rid of his sister and then convince Vanessa to come to dinner with him.

A couple of Charity's girlfriends came bouncing up just as the three of them were almost to the aisle. "Charity, party tonight out at the Kingston Ranch. You've got to come."

Well, didn't that just play right into his hand? Charity beamed him her sweetest smile. "I can get a ride home."

One of the girls batted her eyelashes at him. "I'm driving, Jameson."

"Fine with me. Vanessa and I will manage."

Charity gave Vanessa a sheepish look. "Will you hate me for running off like this?"

Vanessa laughed. "Of course not. You've more than done your duty as my Miss Bronco coach. Go have some fun. I remember those bonfires. Best time ever."

Charity grabbed Vanessa in a hug, then took her by the shoulders. "Okay, tomorrow's the big barbecue. You need to be there by two. I'll be over at one with extra hats. We can double-check your makeup and wardrobe and I'll answer any last-minute questions you might have. And then we'll ride to the park together."

Vanessa suggested, "I think I can manage on my own if you just want to—"

"Nope." Charity put up a hand to punctuate the word. She brought that hand to her chest. "I'm there. You can count on me."

Vanessa grabbed her in a final hug, and then Charity headed off down the row behind her friends.

"Ready, then?" Jameson asked. Vanessa wore a look he couldn't quite read. Did she plan to insist on hitching a ride with someone else—or maybe calling an Uber? The Uber would take a while. Uber drivers in Bronco were thin on the ground.

Not that it mattered. "We've already been through this. You're riding with me." Was that too damn caveman? He softened the command with, "Please?"

The smile she gave him then had him almost believing he might finally be getting somewhere with her. "I was just thinking about how smoothly you defused the situation with those boys. I should be more appreciative. Thank you for doing that." She said it softly, with what sounded like real admiration.

He tipped his hat to her. "It was my pleasure." He wanted to try his luck, take her hand.

But no. They should talk first. He needed her agreement to change the rules she'd laid down on The Night That Really Did Happen, no matter how hard she tried to pretend it hadn't.

"After you." He gestured for her to go ahead of him to the aisle.

It was a scramble, getting out of the parking lot, with everybody leaving the arena at once. They got in line with all the other vehicles.

Once they were out of the lot, she took off her hat and turned to set it on the back seat with the other ones Charity had brought for her to choose from. They'd turned onto the highway into town when she said, "Is there someplace private we could talk?"

Talk? That sounded promising. Maybe they were finally on the same page. "How about a beer?"

She shot him a glance. "At a bar, you mean?"

"I was thinking maybe DJ's Deluxe." The bar there was gorgeous, and they could move to the main restaurant for a nice dinner after he got her to agree to go out with him, to see where this attraction might take them.

Another quick sideways glance from her. Then, "I was thinking someplace quiet, just you and me. The turnoff to Bushwhacker Creek's coming up. Let's go there."

He had a blanket in back and he knew a couple of pretty spots along that creek. "All right."

A few minutes later, he turned onto a dirt road. Not long after that, at a wide bend in the road, he pulled over and parked.

She didn't wait for him to see to her door but got out on her own. He refused to take that as a bad sign. Vanessa Cruise was an independent woman, and he liked that about her almost as much as he wished she would give in and let him treat her the way a man ought to treat his woman.

He took the blanket from the toolbox in back. They set out along the road until they came to the trail that descended to creek side. After a nice stroll along the bank, they came to a tree-shaded spot he particularly liked.

"This looks good," he said.

They spread the blanket and sat down. "It's nice here," she said, her gaze on the clear, rushing water.

He studied her profile, admired the graceful slope of her nose and the inviting fullness of those lips of hers. He loved her freckles, the darker ones visible even today, with the sexy Miss Bronco makeup masking them. One rode the apple of her right cheek. He couldn't see that one at the moment, but he knew it was there, waiting to tempt him when she turned her head his way. As for the small constellation of them closer to her mouth on the left side, those he could touch right now with a brush of his fingers—or better yet, the press of his lips, the swipe of his tongue.

If she would let him.

At this point, he couldn't be sure she would, and that had him hesitating to make his move.

She turned to him. There it was, that lone visible freckle on the apple of her cheek. "I can't help thinking that there's still a lot of summer left." Not near enough, if you asked him. "I'm here till the end of August."

He actively held himself back from touching her. It took serious effort, but somehow, he managed it. So far, at least. "A lot can happen in two months."

"Well, I, um…"

"Yeah?"

"Jameson, I think I need to face facts."

"About…?"

"Well, I keep knocking myself out, trying to make myself forget our one night together…"

Hope burned hot in his chest, but he kept his tone light. "And how's that working out for you?"

She blew out her cheeks with a hard breath. "Not well. Today, at the rodeo, it all kind of came clear to me—that you are a good guy and I enjoy your company and…" She seemed to run out of steam.

He leaned in a fraction closer to her and her scent of roses taunted him. "Say it."

"It's just that I think about you." Her thick, dark brows drew together. Was that longing he saw in her eyes?

He gave her words back to her, meaning every one. "I think about *you*. A lot."

And she smiled with a relieved little sigh. "I kind of thought so."

He couldn't resist teasing her. "Did you think I was trying to hide that I can't stop thinking of you?"

"Um, no."

"Good."

"So then…" She gave a tiny cough into her hand, a stall, really, as she braced herself for whatever she'd been working up to saying. "I was thinking today that, if we were to agree to keep things just between us, why shouldn't we have a little fun together until I leave at the end of August?"

He would have pulled her close right then, except for that last line. "Just between us, you said?"

"Yes. I'm not comfortable with taking it public, but I do want to be with you. I want that a lot. So if you're willing to keep the time we spend together private, not let anyone else know we're seeing each other, I would love to go back to your place with you right now."

"You're saying nobody can know that we're spending time together."

"What?" Her low voice had a definite edge to it now. "I didn't make that clear?"

He needed some distance. Jumping to his feet, he swept off his hat, beat it once on his thigh, put it back on and stared out at the creek until he felt he could speak without yelling at her. "Vanessa, what is up with you?"

"I told you at New Year's. I'm not staying in town, and whatever goes on between us is just for fun and just for now."

He turned to look down at her. "Fine. It's only till the end of August. That doesn't mean we can't have dinner together at a decent restaurant like any other single man and woman who are attracted to each other might do."

She got up, too. They faced each other across the empty blanket. Somewhere in the bushes on the far side of the creek, a meadowlark loosed its high, plaintive song.

"I just don't want my family in my business," she said. "You know how it is around town. If we go out to dinner, people will notice. Word will get back to my mother and my grandmother—and now Winona, too."

"So what?"

"They want me here, at home and happily married. I just don't want them to get their hopes up, that's all."

He'd had enough of the careful distance between them. Stepping onto the blanket, he reached for her hand.

She didn't resist. On the contrary, she came into his arms with a soft, willing sigh. "Vanessa," he whispered into her upturned face, his voice like a growl to his own ears. "You've made me wait too damn long."

She had her soft hands on his chest and her head tipped back at just the right angle. Those beautiful freckles were on full display. "And what am I trying to tell you? I'm saying that you don't have to wait any longer."

He swooped down and took her mouth.

She tasted so good, like all the best things—sweetness and heat, laughter and tenderness. For too long, he'd wondered if those things would ever really be his.

Her right hand strayed upward and wrapped around his neck. He felt her fingers sliding into the hair at his nape, and he took the kiss deeper, gathering her body closer, sense memory firing—the way she felt naked in his arms, strong and so soft, more than enough to grab onto, to *hold* on to. He wanted to take her to the blanket, peel off every stitch of clothing and have her right here, by Bushwhacker Creek, under the late-afternoon sky.

But they still had things to settle between them. He broke the kiss, taking dark satisfaction in her groan of protest as he lifted his mouth from hers. "You don't want your family to get their hopes up about what?"

She gazed at him, her mouth swollen from his kiss, her eyes dreamy and soft. "That I might, um, fall for a local man and, you know, move back home."

He couldn't seem to stop touching her. With the tips of his fingers, he combed the hair back from her temple and asked gently, "I can't believe that they're going to get their hopes up because I take you out to dinner. We all have to eat. Sometimes men and women eat together in a restaurant. It doesn't have to be life changing. It's only dinner. And your mom and your grandma and wise old Winona, they all seem like pretty sharp women to me. They're not going to start planning the wedding just because you're seen around town with me."

She let out a little groan and rested her forehead against his chest. "You're right. I know it." And then she looked up to meet his eyes again. "But I'm not ready to go public with you."

He dropped his arms from around her and stepped back off the blanket. "When, then? When *will* you be ready?"

"I can't answer that. I…" She seemed to catch herself. And then she bit the corner of her lower lip and confessed, "Okay. That's not so. I'm not *ever* going to be ready. I can't do that again. Not now, anyway. Maybe eventually…" She might have used the word *eventually*, but he heard her real meaning in her voice. In this case, *eventually* meant *never going to happen*.

"You can't do what again?"

"Get stars in my eyes. Start thinking that…" Her voice trailed off. She sucked in a deep breath and said, "Jameson, I want to be with you, but it's really not going anywhere beyond the end of August. I don't want to have to talk to my family about how I like you a lot, but it's only for now. I just want you.

I want you and I think you want me and I'm willing to be with you for the summer—discreetly."

"Discreetly. You mean in secret, sneaking around so no one will know."

"Fine. Yes. If you want to put it that way."

He wanted to agree to her terms. He wanted that so bad.

But he also wanted a chance for more.

How could he get more if she wouldn't even say yes to dinner at DJ's Deluxe? "No. That's not good enough." Dropping to a crouch, he swiftly rolled up the blanket. "Come on." He rose and tucked the blanket under his arm. "I'll take you home."

Chapter Five

After Jameson dropped her off at the apartment and drove away without once glancing back, Van found Callie inside at the stove. She'd cued up her favorite country-and-western playlist and she bounced around to Haley Mae Campbell singing "Highway Honey."

"Spaghetti and Italian sausage, anyone?" she asked between verses.

Van longed to grab her and hug her and cry on her shoulder. Instead, she put on a bright face and replied, "Let me wash my hands. I'll cut up the salad."

"I bought a bottle of red."

"We are so livin' large."

"Do the honors and screw off the top? I like my wine to have a chance to breathe."

Twenty minutes later, they sat down to eat.

Callie held up her juice glass of red. "A toast. To you and me and this elegant meal." Van tapped her roomie's glass with hers, and they both drank, after which Callie said, "Whatever it is, you should just tell me. We'll eat our dinner and drink more wine and I will share with you all the wisdom of my twenty-five years."

Van should have known her friend would sense her need to talk. She set down her glass. "It's Jameson."

Callie made a show of widening her big brown eyes. "Shocker."

"As in you're *not* shocked at all?"

"As in when he looks at you—fireworks. And when you look at him? Same. I'm just not getting why you don't follow up on that."

"Long story."

"I understand." Callie's teasing tone had gentled. "A story of three players who broke your heart. And the boring guy you decided to settle for, who ended up dumping you, too."

"Even when you say it kindly, that hurts."

"Am I wrong?"

"No—and that's why it hurts. And just for the record, Donnie Bell really wasn't a player.

At least, he didn't start out as one." Somehow, that had made his screwing her over in front of everyone at Bronco High all the worse.

Really, Donnie *was* the worst. He'd hurt her so deeply, cut her right to the core. Because she had loved him with her whole young, naive heart and soul.

A Bronco Valley native who lived down the street from her growing up, Donnie Bell was the love of Van's life—or so she honestly believed at the time. They were BFFs from early childhood. At thirteen, Van realized she loved him as more than a friend. They shared their first kiss that year, in eighth grade. In ninth grade, they declared their undying love for each other. He asked her to marry him sophomore year. She said yes and he slipped a sterling silver promise ring on her trembling finger. They planned a simple ceremony for right after they graduated from Bronco High.

Handsome and kind, Donnie was all hers. He'd always been all hers. At sixteen, she'd believed in his love absolutely. Donnie Bell would be true until death.

But as he grew up, Donnie's body filled out with muscle, and his smooth face became square-jawed and manly. More than just handsome by then, he was a real heartthrob.

Donnie not only proposed to Van sophomore

year, he also joined the football team. He became a Friday night hero. Still, he had eyes only for Van.

Until senior year.

By then, more than one of the rich girls from Bronco Heights had set her sights on him. Donnie ignored those girls—at first.

But Maura Flannigan wouldn't give up. She was pretty and popular, and her dad had plenty of money. She went after Donnie with single-minded, unwavering determination. In the end, Donnie let her catch him.

He shattered Van's trust as well as her heart and her love for her hometown. By the time he and Maura and her posse of popular girls were through with her, Van couldn't wait to get out. When she left for college, she'd felt nothing but gladness to be moving on, leaving Bronco behind for good.

Callie brushed her shoulder, a fond touch. "I get it. I do. But after Donnie, you didn't give up, did you? You kept trying."

Oh yes, she had. Through David and Chaz and Trevor.

Callie spun pasta on her fork. "I mean it. You can't give up now. You need to give love a fighting chance." She ate the bite of pasta before concluding, "That's what life's all about."

"Ugh."

"That sound?" Callie put on a reproachful glare. "That sound is not the least encouraging."

Van and Callie had spent more than one evening sharing grisly tales of life in the trenches, romance-wise. What Van hadn't said a word about to her summer roomie–turned–BFF was what had transpired on TNTNH. "I have a confession…"

"I love those." Callie picked up the wine and refilled their glasses. "Continue."

Van told her friend everything—about TNTNH as well as all that had gone down by Bushwhacker Creek earlier that evening.

When she finished, Callie said, "You wild thing, you. There we all were at New Year's, hanging out at Happy Hearts eating vegetarian finger food, toasting Evan and Daphne and their forever love, while you were at Wild Willa's hooking up with Jameson John." She offered a high five and they slapped palms. "Way to go, Cruise. That's how you ring in the New Year, if you hear what I'm sayin'."

"You're right. It was wonderful. And he and I both agreed it was just that one night."

"Please. He likes you. You like him. Step outside your comfort zone and give the man a chance."

"A chance? Didn't I just explain that I offered to be with him for the summer and he turned me down?"

"Because you said you want to sneak around."

"Yes, well, I said I wanted to keep it private, but whatever. He said no. So it's over without ever really even getting started. No way he's going to be coming around looking to try again."

"And yet here you are, missing him already. Because you really like him. And when you really like someone, you reach out and try again. I'll say it one more time. Give the man a chance."

Charity breezed in the door at one the next afternoon looking absolutely beautiful, wearing her usual glowing smile. "It's gorgeous out today. The perfect Independence Day—and, Vanessa, you look fabulous. I like that shirt as much as the one yesterday."

"Thank you." Van tried to ignore the elephant missing from the room. But she couldn't quite do it. "Where's Jameson?"

Charity set her makeup kit on the table. "Oh, one of the fences went down out at the Double J, and a couple of steers got out. He'll deal with that and be along later."

"I see. Well, I hope it all, um, works out."

Charity shrugged. "It's a ranch. Fences are bound to go down now and then."

Van took care not to lock eyes with Callie. Her friend knew way too much now. And Van had no doubt they would be discussing the Jameson situation again at some point.

Just not this afternoon, with his sister in the room. Besides, what more was there to say? Her fantasy of a hot, secret summer romance had ended without ever getting started.

End of story. Nothing to see here. Time to move on.

Charity picked up her makeup kit again. "Let's get to it. This won't take long."

Charity, Van and Callie caravanned to the day's Red, White and Bronco festivities.

At Bronco Park, the barbecue experts from all the local ranching families had their smokers and charcoal grills going. The rich, tempting smells of hickory smoke and seared meat filled the air.

Three of Charity's girlfriends came running up. They wanted her to head over to the row of carnival-style booths on the other side of the barbecue area. The girls couldn't wait to dunk last year's high school football hero off his perch and into a giant tub of icy water.

"Go," Van instructed. "I'm on this. Have fun."

"But I should take you to the pie tables." Charity grabbed her hand. "Come on. I'll introduce you to Mrs. Abernathy and Mrs. Brandt. They're heading up the pie contest committee this year."

"I can see the pie tables from here, and I know

both Angela and Mallory. Don't worry. You have taught me well, and I love pie. There is no problem here. Go with your girls. Win a carnival glass bowl or a stuffed giraffe."

Charity hugged her—carefully, so as not to mess up her perfectly arranged hair or knock her red spangled cowboy hat askew. "I'll be back to check on you, just in case you need me…" She was still offering aid and suggestions as her girlfriends dragged her toward the game booths.

"Vanessa! Callie! Over here!" Van glanced toward the sound of her mother's voice. Wanda Cruise waved at them from a picnic table about twenty yards away.

Callie took her arm. "Let's go say hi to your folks."

At the table, Wanda sat with Grandma Daisy and Great-Grandmother Winona. Sean Donohue, Wanda's boyfriend, had come, too. They'd worked together for years, Sean and Van's mom. Shortly before last Christmas, they'd finally come out to the family as a couple. Before that, they'd kept their romantic relationship a secret—which people did now and then for any number of reasons, damn it. Too bad a certain thickheaded rancher refused to see it that way.

"Sit with us," Winona commanded.

Well into her nineties, Winona Cobbs was slender, almost birdlike, with a halo of snow-white hair. She looked frail, and she'd been ill a lot last year when she still lived up north in Rust Creek Falls. Since reuniting with her family, though, Winona had not only miraculously regained perfect health, but she'd also developed a flashy personal style. Today, she wore an electric-green silk shirt and jeans, along with a crystal-bedecked cowboy hat to match.

"You look beautiful, G-G." Van used the pet name she'd chosen a few months before in order not to have to say "Great-Grandmother" all the time. She took the seat next to Winona.

"Thank you, sweetheart." Winona patted Van's knee with her spider-thin, wrinkled hand. "Where's that handsome fella of yours?"

Callie snickered as she slid in on Van's other side. Van shot her a warning glare and turned back to Winona. "G-G, I don't have a fella." Van kept her smile easy and her tone gentle. "I'm a happy single woman, and you know that."

Winona leaned closer, bringing the faint scent of sandalwood and patchouli. Since she'd opened her little fortune-telling enterprise, Winona had switched from light floral perfumes to more earthy essential oils. "Sometimes, sweetheart, you have to lose in order to win."

Van decided not to ask what, exactly, that might mean. A quick change of subject seemed the best way to go. "Where are Evan and Daphne?"

Across the table, her mom shook her head. It was answer enough. From over in the large, open area where the men had the smokers and grills going, Cornelius Taylor let out a loud bray of laughter. Beef was the order of the day, with all the local ranchers competing to win the blue ribbon for Best of Bronco Barbecue. Daphne's dad tended to rule the roost at the Independence Day cook-off—and right now, he and Daphne weren't getting along. Not surprising she'd chosen to sit this one out.

Van's mom had set the table with dishes and flatware she'd brought from home. She'd also brought Tupperware containers full of sides, including fresh, oven-baked rolls. As for the savory main course, barbecue, the family would buy that right here at the park. Wanda, Sean and Grandma Daisy got up together to head for the booths that sold the perfectly cooked meat straight from the smokers.

"Hmm," said Callie. "I think I need to check out the choices while they're still on the grill. Be right back."

Van didn't want to leave Winona all on her own, so she stayed put. G-G regaled her with an update on her new psychic business venture and then sent a meaningful glance toward the barbecue area. "Callie is such a lovely girl…"

"Yes, she is," Van replied with a nod. Over by

the smokers and grills, Van's roomie had struck up a conversation with one of the Abernathy men—Tyler, if Van remembered correctly. He'd been a year or two ahead of Van in school. As Van watched, Callie laughed at something Tyler said, her gaze shifting shyly away and then back, her cheeks a little flushed. Cutest thing ever. With Van, Callie was always frank and straightforward. Sometimes Van forgot that her friend had a shy side.

Winona remarked, "Don't those two look good together?"

Van was just about to agree when Tyler's mom, Hannah, appeared at his side. She had a baby in her arms. With a quick nod at Callie, Hannah passed the baby to Tyler. A moment later, Callie turned to go. Tyler stared after her, but Callie didn't look back.

"She really ought to just ask him," Winona said quietly.

Van frowned at her great-grandmother. "Ask him what, G-G?"

But Winona only jumped lightly to her feet. She started taking the covers off the side dishes. A few minutes later, the others, Callie included, returned with clamshell containers of hot, fragrant barbecue.

Van waited for everyone to settle into the meal and start chatting together before asking her friend in a whisper, "So...? Tyler Abernathy, huh?"

Callie leaned in close and answered for Van's ears alone, "I didn't see his wedding ring until his mom handed him his baby girl—whose name is Maeve, by the way. Maeve is nine months old and, as you might have noticed, completely adorable. Just like her mother, I have no doubt."

Van made a sad face. "Sorry, honey."

Callie grabbed another rib from one of the containers in the middle of the table. "At least the food is the best ever."

Earl Tillson jumped to the stage where the band would play later. He stepped up to the mike there. "May I have your attention, ladies and gentlemen. Once again, Red, White and Bronco is giving you the best barbecue in Montana, courtesy of our local ranchers. The entries have been judged and the competition was fierce, and I'm up here right now to give you your winners."

A wave of applause followed.

Earl announced, "In third place, the Double J!" Everybody clapped as Randall John got up to accept the white ribbon. Taylor Beef came in second. Cornelius strutted to the stage to claim the red, his second-born son, Brandon, at his side.

"And in first place, let's have a giant round of applause for..." Earl drew out the moment before shoving a fist in the air and shouting, "Abernathy Meats!"

It wasn't much of a surprise. For as long as Van could remember, the Taylors and the Abernathys inevitably won the top two ribbons. Still, the applause level rose higher than before as Tyler and his handsome brothers broke out in cheers. Their father, Hutch, stepped up to take the blue ribbon.

But not everyone approved of the Abernathy win. At the next table over, Van heard a man mutter, "Right. Once again, it's the Abernathys and Taylors taking first and second place…"

"Surprising exactly no one," groused the woman beside him.

The complaint was picked up and echoed here and there through the park. One of the Dalton boys, Boone, said right out loud it wasn't fair. A distant Abernathy relation shouted at him to pipe down.

Earl Tillson put an end to the barbecue controversy by announcing, "And now, I want to introduce you all again to our one and only Miss Bronco. Vanessa Cruise, get on up here and say hi to the folks!"

"Yippee," she muttered under her breath as she cleaned the barbecue off her hands with a wet wipe. Rising, Van executed a fancy pageant wave at all and sundry. Everyone applauded as she headed for the stage—which was good. Wonderful, even. At least today no one had questioned her claim to the crown or called her "the fake Miss Bronco."

Not so far, anyway.

Up on the stage, Earl stuck the mike in her face, and she said a few words about the superior quality of barbecue produced by Bronco ranchers and how great it was to see everyone out having a fine time on this gorgeous Independence Day.

"Vanessa," Earl spoke into the mike again. "It's my job to ask you the all-important question…"

"Hit me with it, Earl."

"Are you ready to judge twelve tasty pies created with love and skill and tender care by the best bakers in Bronco?"

"Earl, when it comes to pie, I'm always ready."

"And ain't that what we needed to hear, ladies and gentlemen?"

The park erupted in applause, whistles and catcalls.

Earl waited till the ruckus died down a bit to instruct, "Right this way, Vanessa." He led her to the three pushed-together folding tables decked with patriotic bunting, accented with vases of red, white and blue mums, and crowned with a row of absolutely beautiful pies.

Sometimes the duties of a beauty queen sucked. But judging the Red, White and Bronco Fourth of July pie contest almost made it all worthwhile.

Right then, Charity, carrying her own folding chair, appeared on Van's left.

Van sat in the chair Earl held for her and beamed up at Charity. "Come on, sit right here beside me. Let's get to work."

Such a challenging task, but someone had to do it. Van and Charity took their time tasting each and every pie—some more than once. Just to be sure. They had a great time, laughing together, making a big deal of each offering so that no baker would feel slighted.

A crowd gathered around them, including all the contest entrants and several of Van's Young Adventurers. Everyone laughed and offered suggestions and encouragements as Van and Charity consulted and argued the merits of each pie, with Van always eager to dig right in and take another bite. Charity held her back, reminding her that they had to respect the "physical integrity" of every pie.

"It's important," Charity insisted, "that we don't eat too much of any one pie, in order that enough of every pie remains to take an attractive picture of at least one large and appetizing slice when the winners are declared. You know we'll make the front page of the *Bronco Bulletin*, right?"

Van slung an arm across her favorite runner-up's slim shoulders and leaned close to whisper, "You're not only gorgeous and talented and smart, but you also have way too much integrity, even about pie. I mean, *nobody* has integrity about pie. It's too delicious. We all just want to gobble it right up."

Charity giggled. "I love pie, too." She drew in a big breath and tipped her head at a determined slant. "But we have a job to do here."

And do the job they did, posing with the winners when Earl announced them. First and second place, a lemon meringue and a spiced apple, respectively, went to women who lived in Bronco Valley. One of the Dalton boys claimed third with a perfectly tart strawberry rhubarb. Each winner got enthusiastic applause, and Van heard not a single muttered complaint about the fairness of the judging.

Was it possible that her detractors were getting used to a girl from Bronco Valley wearing the Miss Bronco crown?

"I think that went well," Charity declared with an approving nod once Earl mounted the stage again to remind everyone of all the fun still to come, including music and dancing and fireworks after dark.

Van grabbed Charity in a hug. "Couldn't have done it without you."

"Yes, you could." Charity hugged her back. "But we sure are a great team."

"Let's face it. We rock."

Right then, Charity's friends ran up to sweep her away.

"Coming," Charity promised them, then turned to Van again. "So. You have the Favorite Pet Contest tomorrow at Happy Hearts. I'll be at your apartment at, say, eleven?"

"Just meet me at Happy Hearts, okay? I have Young Adventurers in the morning. So I'm thinking if you could be there by noonish?" The contest started at one.

"See you at noon, then." With a last quick hug, Charity went off to join her friends.

Van watched Jameson's little sister go, her thoughts turning bittersweet. She hadn't spotted Jameson once all day. Had he skipped the barbecue because of her?

Though he'd only turned her offer down yesterday, somehow it felt like she'd been missing him for a long time—missing his sexy smile and that devilish look in his eyes, the look that promised things she shouldn't even let herself think about.

Because where could it go, anyway? Yes, she wanted to spend her summer nights with him. But really, wasn't a secret summer fling just asking for trouble? She'd never been any good at casual relationships. Consider TNTNH as an example. She'd finally indulged in a one-night stand—and then spent way too much time afterward trying not to think about the man she'd shared it with.

What made her imagine she'd suddenly become the kind of woman who wouldn't end up getting attached?

One way or another, she always did. And so far, getting attached had only brought her heartbreak in the end.

"Hello, Nessa." The familiar voice came from behind her—and no, it wasn't Jameson's voice, but the voice of the boy she'd once loved to distraction. The voice she'd once thought she would never grow tired of hearing.

How sad, really, that love could turn into ashes, into nothing but an echo of remembered pain. She didn't even want to look at him.

In the nine years since Donnie Bell decimated her heart, she'd come face-to-face with him twice. Both times, just the sight of him had cut her to the core.

The first time, seven years ago, he'd given her a big, phony smile. He'd behaved as though she was just some girl he knew once and hardly remembered anymore. The second time, four years later, he'd bragged to her about how his father-in-law, who owned two car dealerships, had put him in charge of the larger one in Bronco Heights, where they sold the luxury cars.

That second time she'd run into him, he'd worn

a fake smile, too. And that time was even worse. That time, the fake smile seemed sleazy and he'd had a certain unacceptable look in his eye. She'd felt sick to her stomach thinking he might try to make a pass or something.

If he'd tried that, she would have kneed him in the family jewels without a second thought. In high school, she'd been a lot more trusting. He'd annihilated her heart and then come back for more. She'd believed him when he said he was sorry, that he'd been so wrong, that he loved *her*, that he couldn't live without her and that he and Maura Flannigan were finished.

Van had forgiven him.

And then he'd betrayed her all over again.

Now, she just wanted not to have to deal with him. She considered her next move—walk away without looking back? Or face him for the third time in all these years?

"I just thought I'd say hi," he said.

Her pride won out. Drawing her shoulders up tall, she turned and met the hazel eyes of the boy she'd once trusted completely, the one who was supposed to be her forever.

Not a boy anymore, Donnie still looked good. A little tired, maybe, but strong and tall and handsome. "Donnie. How are you?"

"Fine." His gaze wandered—down over her

body and slowly back up again. "You look beautiful."

She didn't know what to say to that. "What do you want, Donnie?"

A chasm of silence yawned between them. Apparently, he couldn't decide how to answer her question.

Strange how life goes. This time the sight of him brought none of the anguish the mere thought of him used to cause her. And the complete lack of pain she felt at this moment had her realizing that the impossible had finally happened.

She was completely over Donnie Bell. Only an echo of sadness remained.

And that echo? Mostly from the loss of the friendship they'd shared as kids—the two of them a team, a couple of awkward poor kids from Bronco Valley. Kings of West Street, they used to call themselves. They would race their battered secondhand bikes up and down the block, flying so fast they swore no one could catch them.

Down by the narrow creek that ran behind Donnie's house, they'd built a fort of willow branches tied together with strips of bark. In their fort, they would whisper to each other of the things they wanted most. A trip to Disney World and a new bike for him. And for her, a good dad, one who didn't disappear from her life without warning, never to return.

"Just wanted to congratulate you on becoming Miss Bronco," Donnie said at last, drawing her out of the lost world of memory, plopping her down in the here and now.

"Thanks. It's an all-new experience for me, and I'm pretty much playing it by ear."

"Donnie!" a slender, pretty, harried-looking blonde shouted from maybe thirty feet away. Pushing a toddler in a stroller, with a baby in a sling attached to the front of her and a little girl of maybe seven or so running along beside her, Donnie's wife, Maura, came rushing toward them.

The little girl kept tugging on Maura's arm. "Mommy, pink popcorn. I want the pink popcorn."

Maura shushed her and kept on coming. The toddler in the stroller had started to fuss. As Maura pulled the stroller to a stop next to her husband, the toddler squawked louder.

The little girl turned to her father. "Daddy, can you *please* buy me the pink popcorn!"

"Sure, princess," said Donnie. He stroked a big hand down her fine blond hair. "Just give us a minute here."

"Vanessa," said Maura, bending to stick a binky in the toddler's mouth and then straightening up with a tight little smile. "Congratulations—on the Miss Bronco thing?"

"Thank you."

"A lot of people were beyond stunned when Earl called your name the other day. I mean, you didn't even enter the contest, and you never were exactly the beauty queen type, now were you? But you look great. Have you lost weight?"

Vanessa managed not to roll her eyes. "Maura, *you* haven't changed a bit."

"Yes, well, I try to keep fit—and with these three little broncos, what choice do I have? Being a mom's a big job." She frowned. "But you never even got married, did you?"

"Nope. Still single. Somebody has to have all the fun, right?"

Maura narrowed her sharp eyes, most likely trying to decide whether Van had just insulted her. In the end, she simply scoffed and turned to her husband. "Come on, now. We can't stand here forever. My parents are waiting."

Donnie sent Van the strangest look—a little sad. And way too weary for a man of only twenty-seven. "Good to see you, Nessa."

"'Bye, Donnie." Van watched them walk away, the toddler starting to fuss again, the little girl still demanding pink popcorn. Yeah, she really had loved Donnie once. It was young love, fierce and passionate, the kind of love that feels destined to last forever.

But it hadn't lasted. Donnie had betrayed her. Twice.

And now, for the first time in the years since it all blew apart with him, she found she really wanted to let all the hurt go, get past the memory of the mean girls whispering behind their hands, pointing at her, laughing at first—and later writing rotten things on her locker with red nail polish, calling her the worst sorts of names, tormenting her, putting her through the high school version of hell.

Today, for the first time, she felt she could almost forgive Donnie's initial betrayal—the one where he showed up one Wednesday morning for advanced biology with his arm around Maura Flannigan after whispering words of love to Van on Tuesday night.

As for his second, more brutal act of treachery, that one still got to her when she let herself think about it. After that second betrayal, she'd stopped being a laughingstock and become the object of outright scorn and hatred. Forgiveness came harder for that.

But it had all happened so long ago. Better to let the hurt go, wish the man well—maybe not for his sake, but for the sake of those three little kids of his. Innocent children needed a loving dad they could count on.

And who was she kidding? No, Van couldn't completely forgive Donnie yet. But she liked to think she was getting there.

For the next few hours, Van sat with her family, enjoying the brownies and coffee she and Callie had bought from one of the booths. Afternoon faded to early evening, and the first star appeared in the clear Montana sky.

Winona leaned close to her. "Make a wish upon a star, sweetheart."

"G-G, haven't you heard? If wishes were rocket ships, we would have settled the far reaches of the galaxy by now."

Winona chuckled, a dry sound, like leaves rustling together high on a mountaintop where few ever go. "Wishes matter. They shape our dreams. And without dreams, how can we foresee what we need to make happen?"

Van leaned close enough to kiss her soft, wrinkled cheek. "That's beautiful, G-G."

"So then, make your wish."

Van gave in. She closed her eyes and let her wish take form. She did it in gratitude for all she had already—her teaching career, which she adored, a family she treasured, who cherished her right back, and good friends like Callie and Charity—and a couple of her girlfriends in Billings, too.

Dear first star, please send me someone to count on, someone I can trust, someone who will never cheat or walk away. Send me a forever sort

YOU pick your books –
WE pay for everything.

You get up to FOUR New Books and TWO Mystery Gifts...absolutely FREE

Dear Reader,

I am writing to announce the launch of a huge **FREE BOOKS GIVEAWAY**... and to let you know that YOU are entitled to choose up to FOUR fantastic books that WE pay for.

Try Harlequin® Special Edition books featuring comfort and strength in the support of loved ones and enjoying the journey no matter what life throws your way.

Try **Harlequin® Heartwarming™ Larger-Print** books featuring uplifting stories where the bonds of friendship, family and community unite.

Or TRY BOTH!

In return, we ask just one favor: Would you please participate in our brief Reader Survey? We'd love to hear from you.

This FREE BOOKS GIVEAWAY means that we pay for everything! We'll even cover the shipping, and no purchase is necessary, now or later. So please return your survey today.

You'll get **Two Free Books** and **Two Mystery Gifts** from each series to try, altogether worth over **$20!**

Sincerely

Pam Powers

Pam Powers
For Harlequin Reader Service

Complete the survey below and return it today to receive up to 4 FREE BOOKS and FREE GIFTS guaranteed!

FREE BOOKS GIVEAWAY
Reader Survey

1

Do you prefer stories with happy endings?

○ YES   ○ NO

2

Do you share your favorite books with friends?

○ YES   ○ NO

3

Do you often choose to read instead of watching TV?

○ YES   ○ NO

YES! Please send me my Free Rewards, consisting of **2 Free Books from each series I select** and **Free Mystery Gifts**. I understand that I am under no obligation to buy anything, as explained on the back of this card.

❏ Harlequin® Special Edition (235/335 HDL GQ5J)
❏ Harlequin® Heartwarming™ Larger-Print (161/361 HDL GQ5J)
❏ Try Both (235/335 & 161/361 HDL GQ5U)

FIRST NAME	LAST NAME

ADDRESS

APT.#	CITY

STATE/PROV.	ZIP/POSTAL CODE

EMAIL ❏ Please check this box if you would like to receive newsletters and promotional emails from Harlequin Enterprises ULC and its affiliates. You can unsubscribe anytime.

of man—and yeah, I know it's a lot ask, but it's about time, don't you think?

So shoot her. Her greatest hope had not died completely. Somewhere deep down, she still nurtured the dream that she might find the right man for her.

"There now," said Winona. "Didn't that feel good?"

Van leaned her head on her great-grandmother's thin shoulder. "Oh, maybe a little bit."

Winona gave another dry-leaf chuckle. "You're a tough nut to crack, sweetheart. Oh, look. Here comes that dear girl, Charity, with one of her good-looking big brothers."

Did Van's silly heart leap? It might've. It definitely skipped a beat when she turned and met Jameson's sin-blue eyes.

"See, Vanessa," announced Charity, slipping her arm into the crook of Jameson's elbow. "He did come."

"I see that."

"Welcome, you two," said Winona. "Sit with us," she commanded, "for a few moments, at least."

Charity took the empty space next to Wanda.

Wanda offered her the paper plate with the last three brownies on it. "Help yourself."

"Thank you." Charity chose a brownie and took a bite. "Yummy."

As for the blue-eyed devil named Jameson, he sat next to Van. "Looks like this is the only spot left."

Van dared to look straight at him. Wouldn't you know? She'd wished for a good, steady man who would love her forever, and what did she get? Sheer temptation. Did he *have* to be so hot? "I heard you had some fences down over at the Double J."

That wonderful mouth tipped up at the corners. "A couple of pesky heifers knocked out some posts."

"Wait. Charity told me steers were the problem."

Across the table, Charity chimed in, "I said the steers got loose."

"And they did," Jameson agreed. "But those heifers, *they* were the problem. Dawson saw them headbutting fence posts, like they thought they had horns or something. They're a temperamental pair. We should have culled them early on."

"Don't even think about it." Charity glared at him—but then she grinned. "They're funny, those two. They've got personality."

"If that's what you want to call it," Jameson muttered.

"That is exactly what I call it," Charity replied. "And I do have a say about what happens to them. Wasn't I the one who fed them by hand when both their mamas died in that freak April blizzard?"

Jameson wore an obstinate expression. His eyes, though? They sparkled with humor. They also stayed focused on Van. "Charity calls them Frilly and Dilly."

"That's cute," said Van's mom.

"Thank you, Wanda." Charity's smile was both sweet and smug.

Jameson grunted. "Please. Personality is the last thing a breeder wants in a heifer. A good heifer is docile. Calm. A docile heifer eats better than a skittish animal. They put up with handling. They produce better meat and calmer-natured offspring. Breeding only docile heifers can dramatically improve the general temperament of a herd within just a few years."

Van ventured, "Should I even ask what's going to happen to Frilly and Dilly?"

"Well, I had to put my foot down." Charity scowled at her brother. "Nobody is eating my babies, and that's that."

"They'll be moving to Happy Hearts," said Jameson resignedly. "I called Daphne about it today. First thing tomorrow morning, I'll be trucking them over there."

"I'll miss them," said Charity. "But I'm really grateful to Daphne that she's made a place where heifers with personality can find a loving home."

The talk turned to other subjects. Winona invited everyone out to see her at Wisdom by

Winona. She promised support and advice for anything that might be troubling them—no issue too large or too small—at a reasonable fee. Grandma Daisy, an artist who'd once illustrated a famous series of children's stories, shared a couple of funny anecdotes about her favorite students in the art class she taught now at the local senior center.

Jameson sat right there beside Van for a good half hour. She took way too much pleasure in his nearness and tried not to act at all interested in him. That would only get the family on her case. They would start in about how she ought to move home. She didn't need that.

But the clear, cool evening seemed even more beautiful since Charity's big brother had claimed the space at Van's side.

As for Jameson, he seemed happy just hanging out, joining in the easy conversation at the table. And each time Van met his eyes, she felt that secret little thrill shimmer through her.

Too often, love had disappointed her. But attraction? That always felt great. There was nothing so sweet as wanting a guy and knowing that whatever did or didn't happen, he felt the pull, too.

Had he reconsidered the offer she'd made last night?

She couldn't help but hope so.

The shadows lengthened, and nighttime approached. A six-piece local band took the stage over by the portable dance floor erected in the park every year for the barbecue.

Jameson glanced up at the darkening sky. "Time I checked on the folks. Maddox and Dawson can always use another hand loading the cookers."

Charity added, "And there's all the picnic gear to pack up." The two rose to go.

"Thanks for everything." Van gave Charity back her spangled hat.

"Tomorrow," said Charity, settling the hat on her flowing blond curls. "Noon. Happy Hearts."

"Perfect." As Van watched them go, she couldn't help hoping she might see Jameson again that evening.

Meanwhile, Van's mom and grandmother started putting the lids on the Tupperware. Everyone over fifty seemed to think it was time to head home.

Grandma Daisy spoke of watching the fireworks later from the front yard. "I like to head straight to my bed once the last rocket shoots skyward," she said with a tired little smile.

After hugs all around, the older folks went on their way.

Van and Callie sat at the table, enjoying the evening together, until one of the Sanchez boys asked Callie to dance. Van got up, too. She stood on the edge of the dance floor, watching, loving the sound of boots tapping rhythm in time to the music.

Some cowboy she'd never met before moved close. "Dance?"

"I would love to."

They joined the crowded floor for "Boot Scootin' Boogie." When that one was over, another cowboy stepped up. They danced to an old Kenny Chesney song. As that song ended, she thanked him and turned—right into the arms of the man she'd been waiting for.

The band launched into a cover of "Beautiful Crazy."

Talk about a glorious moment. Van closed her eyes and gave herself up to the clear night, the glow of the party lights strung overhead, that first star keeping watch far above and the perfect feel of Jameson's strong arms around her.

"We should talk." His breath was warm in her ear.

"Hmm." She brushed the close-cut hair at the back of his neck, reveled in the feel of his skin under her fingers. So what if love never worked out for her? Heat and magic, passion and tenderness—

on a night like tonight, those felt like more than enough. "Talk? That's what you want from me?"

"To start, yeah."

She pressed her body closer to his. It felt so right when he held her in his arms. All through the long winter, into spring and early summer, she'd missed this.

Missed *him*.

Just one night. That's all they'd had. And yet, she couldn't get the man out of her thoughts.

It's only for now, she reminded herself. *This, between us, it's for the summer and that's all.*

Did her heart listen?

Never mind about that.

She wrapped her hand around the nape of his neck, stroked her middle finger in that tender place behind his ear. "You know I'm interested. I thought I made that clear *last* night."

He nuzzled the hair at her temple. "I love how you smell. Like roses—and something else. Something woodsy, a little sharp."

"Juniper."

"That's it." He breathed deep. "I like it. A lot."

"So you wanted to talk about what shampoo I use?"

He chuckled. The sound vibrated from his body into hers. "I wanted to talk about doing things your way."

Her hopeless heart beat a faster rhythm. "Yeah?"

"Yeah, Vanessa. You still open to that?"

She looked up into those eyes that were deep and dark now, night-blue. "I am, absolutely. I'm open, Jameson. To you."

Chapter Six

Now that he had Vanessa in his arms, Jameson knew he'd made the right decision. He'd lain awake half the night last night, staring at the shadows lurking up near the vaulted ceiling, trying to tell himself that *he* was right and she was wrong, that he'd had enough of trying to get through to her.

But then, a few hours before dawn, he'd finally faced the truth. He wanted to get close to her. And with a skittish woman like Vanessa, a man only had a chance of getting close if he agreed to do so on her terms.

The irony of the situation did not escape him.

He'd spent a lot of years having nothing but a real good time when it came to the fairer sex. When a woman got too clingy or started talking marriage and babies, he couldn't get the hell out fast enough.

And then he finally grew up. He'd started hungering for a family—with the right woman. He'd met Maybelle. They'd married. And from her, he'd learned a painful lesson. In the immortal words of Jon Pardi, "It ain't always the cowboy that rides away."

Would Vanessa have him humming the same tune in the end?

It sure did look that way. But a man could never win if he refused to play the game.

So for now, forget the future. He had Vanessa in his arms, and the way she looked up at him, dark eyes soft and hopeful, promised a great night ahead and, just maybe, if he played his cards right, more nights to come.

Whatever happened, at least he'd have a good time while she remained in town. It wasn't near enough for him. But to have a prayer of more, he needed to stay in the damn game—and keep a check on himself.

She'd made it painfully clear that she had no interest in getting serious. He needed to remember that, needed *not* to get too attached.

And who could say? Maybe they'd grow closer.

Close enough that she'd learn to trust him. Close enough that she'd be willing to change her rules.

Right now, though, he needed not to push her when she refused to budge.

"You want to stay for the fireworks?" Jameson asked as the song ended and another slow one began.

Van pulled back enough to meet his waiting eyes. "Nope. I was kind of thinking I might follow you to your place."

The way he smiled at her made her stomach hollow out and hot shivers race up and down her spine. "Get our own fireworks going?"

She returned his smile. "You just read my mind."

"Damn, woman. I do like the way your mind works."

She wanted to lift up and fit her mouth to his. But there were too many people around who didn't need to know that she and Jameson had plans for the evening—intimate plans.

Apparently, his thoughts followed the same track as hers, because he quirked a dark gold eyebrow and said, "I really want to kiss you now."

She gave him her sternest schoolteacher glare. "But you won't."

A low, rough chuckle escaped him. "Just checking. I want to be sure I'm clear on the rules."

"Simple. Nobody else needs to know, and nobody else *gets* to know."

Something happened in his eyes. He glanced away for a fraction of a second. But then he nodded. "Got it."

"So, I'm thinking you go first. I'll say goodnight to Callie and then I'll be along."

"You remember the way, then?"

"Oh yes, I do."

He pulled her close again. With a contented sigh, she tucked her head under his chin. As they swayed together, he suggested, "Let's just finish out this song."

They held each other close—but not too close—until the song ended.

He whispered, "If you get lost, you call me." And then he was gone.

One of the Dalton boys asked for a dance. It was a fast one. As soon as the fiddle hit the last note, Van went looking for Callie.

She spotted her roomie by the picnic tables and hurried over to say good-night.

When Van reached Callie's side, her friend leaned in close and teased, "So? Nice dance with Jameson?"

Van couldn't hide her grin. "Very nice, thank you."

They shared a long look, and Callie said, "Let

me guess. Things aren't exactly over between you two, after all."

"You are sworn to secrecy. I really don't want anyone in my family to know."

"Haven't you heard? Secrecy is overrated. You're a grown woman. Your family really can't tell you what choices to make."

"I know. But I don't want them hoping and dropping hints and, well, all up in my business in their sweet and loving way."

"I'll say it again. They can't make your choices for you."

"I mean it. Not a word to anyone." She crooked her little finger and held it out to Callie. "Pinkie swear."

Callie groaned, but she hooked pinkies with Van. "Happy now?"

"Very."

"You have a certain look about you. You're meeting him, aren't you?"

"I will say this much. Don't wait up."

When Van pulled her Forester into the driveway at Jameson's house, he was waiting on the front step, his tall frame silhouetted by the inside lights behind him.

Van grabbed her shoulder bag and got out. Shoving the door shut, she ran around the front of the car, eager to get to him. He held out his arms and she jumped into them, laughing, wrapping her arms and legs around him.

Laughing along with her, he spun her in a circle.

In the distance, she heard whistling sounds and a series of loud pops. She pointed skyward, where a streak of red shot high and bloomed into a giant flower of light. "The fireworks have started."

"You'd better believe it." His lips met hers. She opened for him, tasting him, her mind a hot, eager whirl of joy and desire.

His big hands cradling her bottom, he carried her inside, not once breaking their kiss as he crossed the great room, finally letting her slide to her feet when he reached the kitchen. She dropped her purse on the counter chair and grinned up at him.

"I'm so glad you're here." He bent to take her mouth again.

It was another one of those kisses, the endless kind. But he didn't pull her close, and she somehow kept herself from swaying into him. Their bodies a few inches apart, their mouths fused together, they kissed for the longest time.

When he lifted his head, she opened her eyes and gazed up at him, feeling dazed and maybe a little bit delirious.

Then something batted against her boot. She

looked down. A skinny, white-spotted brown dog stared up at her. "I didn't know you had a dog."

"Meet Slim. He's a German shorthair—mostly, anyway. Slim's about a third Weimaraner."

She bent to take Slim's long face between her hands. "Hey, buddy." Slim gazed at her through soulful brown eyes and gave a low, happy whine. His tail slapped the floor as she scratched under his chin and around the back of his ears. "Where were you last New Year's Eve?"

"At the vet's, as I recall. Little run-in with a coyote. Slim won the match, but the coyote got in a lick or two."

She gave Slim a last scratch. Jameson put down a hand, and she took it. A sweet shiver coursed through her as she rose. "I can't believe I'm really here again."

He touched her hair—a careful touch, his palm resting lightly against the curve of her skull. "You want something to drink? A snack, maybe?"

She reached up and brushed her fingers along the sculpted line of his jaw, enjoying the feel of his short beard against her fingertips. "Just you."

He caught her hand. Pausing only to give Slim the command to stay, he led her down the short hall to his room—and kicked the door shut behind him, rousing a memory of that night last winter, of the sheer glory of it. He'd kicked the door shut that night, too.

And she'd promised herself that the wonder she'd shared with him would never happen again. Some promises, apparently, just begged to be broken.

They stood by the turned-back bed in the light of a single lamp. He unbuttoned her shirt and took it away, dropping it on the bedside chair. Quickly, he got rid of the rest of her clothes—or most of them, anyway.

He pushed her down to sit on the side of the bed, knelt at her feet and removed her boots and her socks. Taking her hand, pulling her upright again, he took down her jeans and her panties, spinning them on a finger before tossing them on the bedside chair.

"Lie down," he commanded.

Without a stitch on, she stretched out on the cool sheet. "Your turn."

Took him about a minute and a half. Boy, did he look good naked. Since last New Year's, her memories of him without his clothes had filled her fantasies and carried her to her happy place a whole bunch of times. But her memories had nothing on the reality of him—so beautifully manly, everything broad and hard and cut.

As he came down to her, she reached up and put her hand flat against his chest. He felt so good—the silky heat of his flesh and beneath that, the strong, steady beat of his heart.

"I missed you," he whispered, as his mouth came down to capture hers.

He settled his body over hers, and her need became frantic—to get her hands all over him, to kiss him long and deep and thoroughly, to give herself up to each thrilling sensation.

She needed to get her hands all over him, and he seemed equally eager to touch her everywhere. They laughed together, rolling from one side of the big bed to the other, hands stroking, grabbing, holding, her long hair tangling all around them.

He cupped her full breast in a big hand, positioning it for his mouth, and then he claimed it, sucking, nibbling—biting, too. She moaned and gathered him tight against her as his other hand strayed down. Outside, far in the distance, she heard fireworks exploding.

"So wet, so ready…" He lifted his head from her breast and took her mouth again.

"Condom," she commanded against his parted lips. "More foreplay later. Right now, I can't wait."

He didn't hesitate. Sticking out a muscular arm, he caught the knob of the bedside drawer and pulled it open. She helped, taking the pouch from his hand, quickly peeling it open, then pushing him onto his back and straddling him.

"You're so beautiful." He stared up at her, eyes glittering, face intent, his fine mouth slightly parted, big chest expanding with each ragged breath. "Like that painting of Venus by that Italian guy."

"Botticelli?"

"Yeah, that one. So soft and full and gorgeous."

She bent for a quick kiss before rolling the condom down over his hard, thick length. "There."

He took over. Big hands clasping her hips, he rolled her under him. She watched his face, loving the heat in his eyes, the strong set of his jaw. He eased his thick, powerful thighs between her soft ones, nudging her legs wider, making room, reaching down to line himself up with her.

"Eyes up here, on me, Vanessa." He growled the words.

She obeyed, lifting her chin and meeting his unwavering gaze.

He thrust in.

She let out a deep groan of pure pleasure as he filled her. "It's been too long."

"Tell me about it."

And then she was grabbing for him, pulling him down to her, wrapping her legs around him, meeting each stroke, her body quickly rising, heat racing down her spine, blooming outward in a sudden, powerful climax.

"So fast," she moaned. "I'm going over…"

"Right there with you." He surged in deep and she felt him, pulsing inside the condom, joining her in a free fall off the edge of the world.

For a few minutes, they simply lay there, panting, holding on to each other.

When he got up to dispose of the condom, he commanded, "Don't even move. I'll be right back."

He wasn't kidding. Two minutes later, he rejoined her on the bed. "Come here." Pulling her good and close, he settled his mouth over hers.

The ecstasy started all over again.

Much later, he tugged the covers up around them.

"It's after midnight," she said. "I should go."

Canting up on an elbow, he smoothed her tangled hair out onto the pillow. "Stay for just a little while."

She reached up, traced the straight lines of his eyebrows, skated a finger down the bridge of his commanding nose. "Not for long."

He dropped a kiss on her chin. "What time do you have to be at Happy Hearts in the morning?"

"Eight at the latest. I run my science workshops from nine to noon."

"If you just stayed here with me, you could—"

She silenced him with the tips of two fingers. "Can't. I have to pull it together in the morning, full-on hair and makeup, all that, because I need to be Miss Bronco in the afternoon. Your sister will be there, checking my look. She's the best, and I refuse to let her down."

"You won't let her down. You couldn't." He kissed her fingertips, caught a thick lock of hair and guided it tenderly behind her ear. "You're beautiful just the way you are."

She let out a low, happy laugh. "Flatterer."

"God's honest truth." He gazed at her so intently.

Sometimes, when he looked at her, she felt… untethered, somehow. Free of all the everyday limitations that held her anchored to the earth. She felt she could sprout wings and fly, go anywhere— even come back home. That she could shed all her doubts and fears, forget the pain she'd suffered in this town, put aside the hard lessons she'd learned in her life. Sometimes he made her feel that she could safely give herself up to him, trust that he wouldn't hurt her, see where this magic they shared might take them.

But no. She wouldn't do that. Donnie and David and Chaz and Trevor had schooled her but good. The fifth time would not be the charm— not now, anyway, and definitely not with a man who lived in Bronco. She accepted that.

Maybe someday she would follow through when she wished on the night's first star. Not any time soon, though.

This, with Jameson, was just for the summer.

She would love every minute with him and go back to her real life in Billings when summer ended.

"Hey," she whispered.

He bent close, rubbed his nose against hers, pressed a featherlight kiss between her eyebrows. "Yeah?"

"I have to go in an hour. Kiss me like you mean it. Let's not waste a minute."

"My pleasure." He claimed her mouth.

She twined her arms around his neck and gave herself up to the moment.

Much to Jameson's satisfaction, Vanessa stayed later than she planned. Like their night last winter, they fell asleep in each other's arms. But unlike that last time, this time he woke when she left the bed.

He turned on the light and watched her get dressed, watched her cover that curvy, beautiful body he would never get tired of looking at. "Don't forget your other sock, now."

She picked it up off the rug, waved it at him and sat on the bed to pull it on. Her boots came last. She stood. "See you."

"I'll walk you out."

She protested that it wasn't necessary, but then she lingered, watching him through heavy-lidded eyes as he grabbed last night's Wranglers and put them on.

Slim was waiting just outside the door.

"Hey, boy." Vanessa knelt to give the mutt a last scratch behind the ears.

And then she headed for the kitchen where she'd left her shoulder bag. Pausing there at the counter, she took out her contacts and put on a pair of tortoiseshell glasses, turning to wink at him as she grabbed up her bag. "I'm out of here."

He stepped in close, blocking her way to the door. "I like those glasses."

She gave him a look, like he'd better not try keeping her here too long. "Um, thank you?"

"They make you look seriously sexy. And also like a really good teacher who won't let her students get away with anything."

"That's me—but with wiggle room. In my class, everybody gets second chances."

He took a lock of her hair and tugged on it. "I'll be at Happy Hearts early to drop off Charity's heifers."

"Maybe I'll see you."

He couldn't stop wanting to touch her. Lowering his mouth to hers, he brushed a slow kiss across her soft lips. "Oh, you'll see me. I think I'll just hang around, help Daphne out with whatever needs doing. I think I should be there for the pet adoption. After all, it's the final Red, White and Bronco event for this year. Wouldn't want to miss that."

"I would like it if you were there."

"That settles it, then."

Her dark eyes had that gleam in them. They made him think of her, in his bed, without a stitch of clothing separating them.

He kissed her again. He just couldn't get enough of kissing her. "Tomorrow night…"

"Jameson, it's already tomorrow."

"Tonight, then. Be with me tonight."

She hesitated. He dared to breathe again when she decided in his favor. "All right. Tonight, then."

"I'll grill us some steaks."

"Sounds good."

"Be here at six?"

"Works for me."

He shouldn't push his luck. But he did it anyway. "I want every night, all through July and August. Every night you'll give me—maybe some days, too. If you're not teaching your workshops, if I don't have fences down, if you've got time to spare."

She laughed. He drank in the sound. "The whole idea is it's just for the summer. And we play it by ear."

"I'm aware." *Two months*. It wasn't enough. Now he just needed to make her see that. He tugged on the pointy collar of her fancy Western shirt. "Can't blame a man for trying."

She laid her hand on his chest and lifted up to kiss him again. "I really do need to go."

Reluctantly, he stepped aside. He and Slim followed her out. Slim at his feet, he stood on the porch waving as she backed out and drove off.

When he looked down at Slim, the dog whined, a questioning sound. "All right. Go on. Take care of your business and let's get some sleep."

Callie, all dressed and ready for work, was sitting at the table sipping coffee and reading the *Bronco Bulletin* when Van finished showering, putting on her makeup, getting dressed and fixing her hair just so. Being a beauty queen entailed way too much grooming, in her humble opinion. She'd run through her limited wardrobe of Miss Bronco–worthy Western shirts, so she'd recycled the shirt she'd worn to the rodeo.

"There's coffee," Callie said. "And you're going to need some more sparkly shirts."

"Yeah." Van poured herself a mug. "Lucky for me, this is the last event I've got to attend in my official capacity till the end of the month. I'll make time before then to go shopping, maybe go hog wild and get some showy hats and cool boots, too." She sipped coffee and lifted the cover off the plate Callie had left on the counter. "Yum. French toast."

"Figured you might be hungry."

"Have I told you lately that I love you?"

"Love you, too. Eat your breakfast. Don't be late."

"Yes, Mother." She joined her roomie at the table and dug in. "So good. Thank you."

"Mmm-hmm. Have a nice time last night?"

"I had a wonderful time."

"Good." Callie turned the newspaper around so Van could see the front-page news. The headline read, A Miss Bronco Like No Other.

The picture showed Van onstage Friday in her old jeans and T-shirt, her hair in a messy bun, wearing her winner's banner, looking faintly bewildered as last year's Miss Bronco placed the crown on her head. "Like no other, indeed."

"Face it. You're a star."

Van loved teaching high school science. But this summer, she had tweens and early teens in her science, technology, engineering and mathematics workshop—and they were a whole lot of fun.

DIY bottle rockets thrilled them. She'd had the kids collecting two-liter plastic pop bottles since day one. Last week, they'd made the launch pads, which consisted of small sections of two-by-four with a cork nailed to the center of each one.

In the barnlike shed that Daphne had provided for their summer classroom, Van gave a short recap lecture on the chemical interaction between vinegar and bicarbonate of soda.

"Bakers often mix the two in their recipes," she said. "Vinegar and soda are also useful in home-made cleaning products. In both cases, you have other, neutral substances to contain the interaction. Substances like…?"

The kids shouted out answers. "Flour!"

"Soap!"

"Correct. Last week we mixed vinegar and baking soda and poured the result into a wide open container surrounded by a small mountain of sand. We watched how carbon dioxide rose to the top of the mixture, creating bubbles and foam that looked like…"

"A volcano!"

"That's right! Today, we make our bottle rockets. With a bottle rocket, you're confining the chemical reaction in the restricted space of the bottle with only a small opening for possible escape, causing the chemical interaction to do what?"

Several of the boys made exploding sounds, while Emma Bledsoe called out, "Vinegar and baking soda make carbonic acid, which decomposes into carbon dioxide gas. The tight space and small opening are what blows the bottle off the cork." Not only a fighter for equal rights in the Miss Bronco beauty pageant, Emma was also a budding scientist.

"Exactly," said Van. "And that makes…"

"The rocket!" crowed more than one of the boys.

They all filed outside to the cleared area in front of the classroom shed and went to work setting up the rocket assembly stations—including the empty bottles with colored tape and markers to decorate them, water and vinegar in measured amounts, baking soda that had to be carefully rolled up in sections of paper towel. And finally, the launching pads with their nailed-on corks.

More than one of the kids had made DIY bottle rockets at home as a family project. Van put one of those students in charge of each station, with Emma running the launching pad station, where the final step had to be done quickly, inserting the nail-mounted cork in the prepped bottle, turning it over to set the launch pad on the cleared space designated for takeoff—and then stepping back fast.

A few of the bottles failed to launch. But most of them soared skyward, sixty feet on average, a few as high as a hundred. It was quite the show. They quickly acquired an audience that broke into applause and whistles each time one of the homemade rockets took off into the sky.

Van spotted Charity in the group of spectators, with Jameson right behind her. She gave them each a big smile, lingering maybe just a little too long on the handsome cowboy with the killer blue eyes and close-cropped, dark gold beard. He actually winked at her, and she tried to ignore the thrill that surged through her in response. She longed to run to him, breathe in the manly scent of him, offer up her mouth for a long, sweet kiss.

Pheromones, she reminded herself. Sexual attraction. No. Big. Deal.

She laughed. He was such a charmer and, really, she couldn't wait for tonight, just the two of them at his place, sharing dinner followed by a whole other kind of sharing, naked in his bed...

And, oops. She needed *not* to stare at him with her tongue hanging out when surrounded by a crowd. The two of them having sex with their eyes in public had to stop or more people were bound to figure out that they'd agreed to make the most of their summer nights—together.

She dragged her gaze back to the cleared space as another bottle rocket achieved liftoff. Too bad she couldn't keep herself from glancing his way again a few minutes later. That time, her gaze snagged on Charity. Jameson's sister was staring right at her, a pensive expression on her pretty face.

No way, Van decided. Charity knew nothing. And from now on, Van would be more careful about where she let her gaze linger.

Clapping her hands to get her Young Adventurers' attention, she praised their creativity, growing knowledge and hard work, thanked their impromptu audience—and instructed the class to get going on cleanup.

Half an hour later, Van sat on a stool in Daphne's small spare bathroom as Charity primped Van for the fast-approaching Bronco's Favorite Pet Contest.

Daphne stuck her head in the door. "Half an hour to showtime."

Charity replied, "We'll be ready, no worries."

"Missed you yesterday," Van said.

Daphne gave a tiny, resigned shrug. "Maybe next year."

"Hope so." Van gave her friend and future sis-in-law a warm smile.

Daphne tapped her knuckles on the door frame. "Well, I'd better get out there, see how it's going." She left them.

"She okay?" Charity asked.

"She's amazing. But, you know, family problems…"

Charity nodded and didn't probe further.

Van asked, "So how did it work out with Frilly and Dilly?"

"Daphne had us put them in a pasture out beyond the hay barn with a bunch of ancient cows that Daphne said are rescues, too. I warned her that my heifers can be troublesome. She said not to worry. The cows and the heifers would work it out. When we left them, Dilly and Frilly were grazing side by side with the elderly cows, looking perfectly content in their new home."

"Glad to hear it."

Charity smoothed Van's eyebrows with a brow gel wand—and asked the big question. "So, you and Jameson...?"

Busted. Van didn't want to lie—not to anyone, really. But especially not to this sweet and generous girl.

She evaded instead, with a vague wave of her hand and a nebulous question. "What do you mean?"

Charity tipped Van's chin up with a finger and brushed on cheek color. "Not going to talk about it, huh?"

Rather than lie again, she said, "Well, it's complicated."

And Charity put down her blusher brush. "I *am* nineteen, you know. I've been to college—yeah, only freshman year so far, but that counts. I've been in love and I've had my heart broken. I like you, and I love my big brother..." Her smooth brow crinkled with a thoughtful little frown. "And what am I getting at here? That I do know a little about what goes on between women and men. For instance, I know that when people say, 'It's complicated,' they're in some kind of semi-relationship that they don't want to talk about."

Now Van felt like a complete jerk. She moaned and dropped her head to the little counter next to the sink.

Charity yelped, "No smearing!"

Van popped back up straight. She'd left a smudge of powder foundation on the edge of the counter. "Sorry."

"It's all right." Charity grabbed the kabuki brush she'd been using earlier and dabbed at Van's forehead. "There we go. Good as new."

"Listen…"

"Hmm?"

"It's just, well, I *do* like your brother." She liked Charity, as well—liked her too much to keep lying to her by omission. "I like Jameson a lot and I'm going to spend time with him over the summer."

That radiant smile of Charity's bloomed wide. "Ha. I knew it."

I just…" She fumbled for the right words and settled for, "Okay, I'll be honest with you. I don't want my family to know that I'm seeing Jameson."

Charity put the brush down. "Do I get to ask why?"

"Of course." Van explained what she'd already explained to Jameson and Callie—that her family wanted her married to a local guy and living in town, and that wasn't going to happen. "I don't want them getting ideas that I might move back to Bronco."

"So what if they do get ideas? Isn't that their problem?"

Van almost face-planted on the counter again. "Sometimes I can't believe you're only nineteen."

"Because I'm right. Am I right?"

"Yes, if they can't accept that I get to make my own life decisions, it *is* their problem. But I don't want to disappoint them. At the same time, I feel awful that I resent them a little. They try so lovingly to run my life."

Van hovered on the brink of saying more, about what had happened in high school, about how she'd hurt her mother and Grandma Daisy and Evan, too, when things went from bad to worse—hurt them with worry for her. She'd kept her suffering to herself. But they'd known there was more going on with her than she ever told them about. And when they'd tried to get her to open up about the awful things she was keeping from them, she'd lied and said there was nothing.

She'd held on to her pride. It had felt like all she had left. She'd wanted to handle the problem all by herself. And she had.

But Charity didn't need to hear that old horror story. And Van didn't want to go there, anyway.

"Let me ask you this," said Charity. "What if, say, things go really well between you and Jameson this summer and he decides that he might be willing to move to Billings?"

"That's not going to happen. He's a Bronco rancher, through and through."

"But just say theoretically—"

"Stop. It's for the summer and that's it."

"Because you like Jameson, but you don't like him *that* much?"

"Your brother is wonderful, he really is."

"Then what's the problem?"

She thought of Donnie and the awfulness of the way he'd dumped her—twice. Of what Maura and her girlfriends had put her through.

Maybe she'd developed something of a neurosis around the whole idea of ever moving home. Or maybe it was simply that, as much as she longed for love, right now she needed to protect her heart. Keeping the thing with Jameson a secret and putting a time limit on it had the effect of constantly reminding her that it was just for now. It kept her from getting serious.

She met Charity's gaze. "I like my life the way it is, you know?"

"Relax your lips. Good." Charity set to work

with a lip brush. "So, being single in Billings, that's a big thrill?"

Van couldn't suppress a snort of laughter at that one.

"Smeared it—and that was my bad. I shouldn't have asked you a question while trying to apply your lip color." Charity dabbed at the corner of Van's mouth with a round cosmetic pad. "And as for my question itself, sorry."

"For what?"

"I kind of insulted Billings, and I get that you like it there."

"Uh-uh. Don't be sorry. We're friends. You get to say to me what you really think."

"Okay, let's try this again." Charity commanded, "Hold still, lips parted—I mean it this time. Don't move." Neither of them spoke as Charity stroked on Van's lip color. "Perfect." She stepped back an inch or two in the limited space. "Jameson really likes you. I can tell."

Van answered honestly. "And I really like *him*."

Charity blew out her cheeks with a hard breath—a very un-Charity-like action. "Well, okay. I just want you to know. He's a good guy, and I would love it if you two got together in a permanent way, and I—"

"Charity, honestly. How many ways can I say that's not going to happen?"

Charity showed her the hand. "Excuse me, Miss Bronco. I was not finished speaking."

"You're right. Sorry. Please continue."

"Thank you, I will. I just want you to know that Jameson is someone you can count on. Someone you can trust."

Van almost scoffed at that one. But then she thought twice.

True, Van used to have a certain idea of him, an idea based on what she'd heard of him years ago. Back then, they all said that he liked a good time, but he didn't get serious with any girl. Really, though, those had only been rumors. She hadn't *known* him then. He'd been three or four years ahead of her in school, a popular, good-looking older boy from a well-to-do family, someone all the girls her age crushed on.

She needed to stop judging him by what she'd heard about him growing up. If everyone judged Van by old rumors, they would probably view her the way Maura seemed to—as someone trashy and dangerous, someone who wouldn't hesitate to try to steal her man.

"Vanessa," said Charity sternly. "Stop scrunching your forehead. You'll get wrinkles."

Van laughed. "A few wrinkles never hurt anyone."

"Maybe not. But as rule, Miss Bronco is never

wrinkled. Her wardrobe *and* her skin are always pristine."

"It's a whole new Miss Bronco nowadays, and don't you forget it. She could be anyone, a regular girl—even someone's single grandma."

"Of course she could be anyone. But this year, she's you. And a smooth brow is prettier. Given a choice, you might as well be pretty." Charity closed up her makeup kit. From the hook on the back of the bathroom door, she took the gorgeous, spangled hat she'd brought from home. "Here, now. Hold your hat and let me fix your hair." Van sat up straight, cradling the hat on her knees, keeping still as Charity fussed with her hair. "Okay, hat, please."

Van handed it over, and Charity set it just so on her head.

"There." Charity studied the final effect. "Perfect. My work here is done. You're ready to wow them."

Van spun on her stool and grinned at herself in the mirror. "Bronco's Favorite Pet Contest, here I come."

Chapter Seven

Van and Charity walked out together to join the day's festivities. Held in a pretty, rolling pasture dotted with alder and burr oak trees, Bronco's Favorite Pet Contest had drawn a good crowd.

"It looks great," said Charity, and then she went to join Jameson, who'd saved her a seat.

Van agreed with Charity's assessment. Daphne had gathered her minions—kids of all ages who volunteered at the pet sanctuary, as well as any spectators who happened to show up early. They'd all pitched in to set up folding chairs in rows. They'd hung flags and red, white and blue bunting from every available tree, booth or bit of outdoor furniture, including the judges' table, the trophy display, the refreshment area and around the podium. Now, they'd all taken their seats, many with pets of their own.

Van took the front-row seat reserved for her and watched as Daphne's many young helpers, more than half of them summer camp Young Adventurers, emerged from the nearest barn with pets on leashes and leads, in carriers and cages. Everyone applauded as the kids brought out cats and dogs, several pigs, a few goats, more than one exotic bird, and various small, furry creatures, too. Van spotted a ferret, a family of hamsters and a large number of rabbits. The helpers and their charges formed a wide arc behind the podium and the trophy display.

Daphne stepped up to the podium. She thanked everyone for coming and reminded them that all Happy Hearts pets were either rescues or animals born right there at the sanctuary.

"Each of these loving fur babies is available to you and your family. I hope you'll consider giving one or more of them a caring, forever home." She swept out a hand to a couple of teenagers seated at the table with the big sign that read Adoption Center. "Toby and Allison are ready to help you adopt the favorite pet of your choice—and now let's get the contest underway."

Daphne went on to introduce the five judges,

after which she grinned at Van. "I'm going to need a little help handing out the trophies and ribbons, so I want to introduce you all to my dear friend and soon-to-be sister-in-in-law. Ladies and gentlemen, youngsters and pets, let's give a big welcome to our own Miss Bronco! Show her some love with a round of applause!"

Everyone clapped some more, and one or two whistled as Van got up, waved to the crowd and went to join Daphne at the podium.

For the next three hours, Daphne introduced each category and Van passed out the trophies. Spectators brought their pets forward to compete, and the helpers did the same with the Happy Hearts animals.

The categories of competition changed depending on the species. Cats got points for qualities like dignity and mesmerizing eyes. Dogs were judged on friendliness, best bark and willingness to chase and fetch a ball. The usual animal-competition traits of obedience and conformation didn't even get a nod. Furry friends at Happy Hearts tended to march to their own individual drums, and few of them had pedigrees. Prizes were plentiful—for the pets brought from home and the Happy Hearts rescues.

A white mutt named Maggie became the star of the day. A border collie/Australian shepherd mix with a brown spot on one eye that reminded

Van of a pirate's eye patch, Maggie barked with the best of them and wagged her tail a lot. She perked her floppy ears and tipped her head sideways when spoken to, as though amused by the humans who surrounded her. She chased a ball when her helper threw it, returning it—not to the helper, but to a little boy and girl in the second row.

"Mommy, Maggie loves us!" cried the little girl as she knelt in front of her chair to give the mutt a hug.

"Daddy, she wants to be with us," said the little boy, gazing up at his father, hopeful and so sweetly serious.

The parents put their heads together, and Maggie found her home. Rising, the mom headed for the adoption table. Everyone clapped and shouted encouragements as she filled out the papers.

More rescued pets found homes as the contest continued. No one was surprised when the grand prize went to Maggie. When Van tied a big blue ribbon around Maggie's neck, spectators, helpers and judges alike burst into boisterous applause.

After that, Daphne encouraged them to stroll around the farm where more loving animals waited to find a good home. She offered coupons for discounts on pet supplies available at the Happy Hearts store and a discount card for microchipping at any local vet.

More spectators lined up at the adoption table, checkbooks and credit cards ready. Happy Hearts Animal Sanctuary didn't charge for adoptions, but new owners paid for the veterinary care already provided to the animals they chose. Many made generous donations to the sanctuary, as well.

"Bronco's Favorite Pet Contest is a hit," Van said to Daphne in a quiet moment when it was only the two of them not far from the podium.

Daphne nodded. "I'm pleased. So many of our residents have found new homes today— and everyone does seem to be having a really good time."

"A fabulous time," Van agreed. She heard a musical trill of laughter. It was Charity, flirting with one of the college boys who volunteered to help out a few hours a day in the summer.

"Charity John's a sweetheart. And her big brother Jameson set out half the folding chairs and helped assemble my new trophy display." Daphne gave a dip of her head toward the now-empty display, where Jameson and Evan stood with their heads together.

Talking about what, exactly? Van couldn't help wondering.

Innocuous man things, no doubt, she reassured herself. After all, Jameson had given her his word not to tell anyone that they were seeing each other. He knew she didn't want her family to know. No way he would tell her brother that they couldn't keep their hands off each other.

Van asked, "When did Evan get here?"

Daphne gave a half shrug. "Around eleven. He pitched in setting up, too."

Again, Van reminded herself that Jameson wouldn't say a word to her brother about the two of them. Still, her palms felt sweaty and her pulse raced. She was about to march over there and see what the two of them were talking about when a cry went up from near the refreshment tables.

"Maggie!" cried the little boy who'd adopted the white dog. "Come back!"

"Don't run away!" the little girl pleaded. "We love you! We want you to come home with us!"

Van glanced toward the shouting in time to spot the grand prize winner racing off, headed for a stand of cottonwood trees and the hills beyond them.

Evan yelled, "We'll get her!" He and Jameson took off at a run. They jumped in Jameson's truck and kicked up a cloud of dust heading down the dirt road that cut through the cottonwoods.

Over by the tables, the two little kids had tears running down their cheeks. Their parents knelt beside them, trying to comfort them.

"I'll go see what I can do," Van volunteered.

"I'll come with you." Daphne fell in step beside her, but two teenage boys came running up with a whole new emergency.

"That mare with the bad attitude stepped on Brian's foot," one of the boys said. Van remembered Brian—a lanky high schooler, sweet-natured and prone to daydreaming.

"I've got the Maggie crisis," Van offered.

"I'll be right there," Daphne promised the boys. "Let me get the first aid kit."

Van ran toward the group of people gathered around the young family with the two sobbing kids. She worked her way into the center of the crowd.

"Miss Bronco, our Maggie ran away." The little girl sniffled and rubbed at her wet eyes with a soggy-looking tissue.

"Don't worry. The search party has already mobilized." Did Evan and Jameson qualify as a search party? Well, there were two of them and they were searching, so why not?

The little boy mumbled, "Wh-what's *mobilize* mean?"

"It means the search party is out looking for Maggie. I'm sure they'll be back with her before you know it."

"I miss her already!" cried the little boy.

"Me, too," the girl chimed in. "I miss her so much!"

Distraction seemed the best option at this

point. Van suggested, "While we wait, why don't we visit the kitten barn?"

Both kids stopped sobbing. They blinked up at her through wide, wet eyes. The little girl sniffled. "Are there a *lot* of kittens?"

"Yes, I believe that there are."

Van led the kids and their parents to the cat barn. After a half hour in the kitten enclosure, the parents decided to adopt a sweet twelve-week-old gray tabby. By then, the children had stopped sobbing, at least. They were still worried about Maggie but smiling through their tears at the idea of bringing a new kitten home.

One of Daphne's helpers provided a cardboard cat carrier, and the family set off for the adoption table once again. Van stood watching just outside the cat barn as Jameson and Evan met them halfway. Maggie the dog was nowhere to be seen. Both men shook their heads sadly as they spoke to the young family. Even from several feet away, Van could hear the regret in their voices.

The little boy opened the top of the carrier so that the men could admire the kitten.

When the family set out again toward the adoption table, Jameson and Evan came toward her.

"No Maggie, huh?" she asked them.

"Sorry," said Jameson.

Evan gestured toward the stand of trees where Maggie had disappeared from sight. "We thought we might catch up with her in those cotton-woods."

"But she was long gone when we got there." Jameson took off his hat and slid it back on again.

"That dog can run." Evan put his arm around Van and gave her shoulders a squeeze. "But the parents are talking about getting flyers out around town. I doubt Daphne can scare up a picture of Maggie, but a description on the flyer might work."

Van couldn't stop looking at Jameson. The warmth in his eyes tempted her. She wanted to go to him, feel his strong arms gather her close in a hug.

But that couldn't happen. She needed to watch herself, not give herself away.

Fun, she reminded herself. *We're just having fun.*

"Where's my girl?" asked Evan.

Van explained about the injury at the horse pasture, and Evan left to find Daphne.

"You okay?" Jameson asked. He took off his hat again and hit it on his thigh.

"Yeah, just... I hope that dog is all right."

"I'm sure she is. She'll either wander back here to Happy Hearts or someone will find her. A lot of people will remember her after today. One way or another, those kids will get their dog back." He put his hat on again.

They stared at each other. She wondered if he wanted to touch her as much as she wanted to throw herself into his arms.

Finally, he seemed to shake himself. "I need to head back to the Double J. I'll say goodbye to Daphne and get a move on. See you at six?"

Her heart lifted a little. Tonight it would be just the two of them. She could touch him at will. "I'll be there."

Once he disappeared behind the next barn over, Van straightened her shoulders and went looking for Charity, but one of the helpers said Jameson's sister had left with a couple of her girl-friends as soon as the contest ended.

In the ranch house, Van found her brother and Daphne canoodling in the kitchen. "Okay, you two. Get a room."

Daphne laughed and turned in Evan's arms. He kept those arms firmly around her, linking his hands at her waist. "This is my house," she said, "so technically we've got *all* the rooms."

Van scoffed. "A likely excuse. What happened at the horse pasture?"

"Brian wasn't paying close attention and the mare, Prudence, decided to mess with him. What can I say about Prudence? She's a troublemaker. But she always causes problems in a conscientious kind of way. Today, she didn't really stomp on Brian's foot so much as put her hoof on it and press down."

"Yikes!"

"He's okay, bruised but otherwise unharmed. I sent him home with instructions to keep it elevated. He'll use an ice pack on it and take it easy for a few days."

Evan bent and nuzzled Daphne on the side of her neck. She giggled like a giddy schoolgirl.

Sometimes Van wanted to ask Daphne what she'd done with her *real* brother. Evan used to be a lot harder to get along with. He had trouble keeping assistants at Bronco Ghost Tours, he was so tough on them. Not anymore. He got along great with Callie now and he catered to Winona, giving her whatever she wanted for her fortune-telling project, always ready to help her change this or move that.

"Clearly you two could use some alone time," she said to the lovebirds. "I'm out of here."

"See you tomorrow," Daphne called after her.

Van waved without looking back.

"Your mom's marinating tri-tips," coaxed Jameson's dad.

It was ten minutes of six and Jameson hoped to get rid of the old man before Vanessa drove up. "Thanks, Dad. I've got steaks of my own to grill."

"They'll keep for a day or two. Come on over, have a beer with me and the boys."

"Not tonight."

Randall opened his mouth to keep trying, but the sound of tires crunching gravel had him turning to see who had just driven up.

Vanessa's silver Forester sailed toward them. Jameson half expected her to drive right on by once she spotted his dad, but she turned into the driveway, after all.

Randall said, "Why, that's Vanessa Cruise," as she got out of the car, circled the front of it and approached the steps. She'd traded her studded snap-front shirt and dress boots for sandals and a silky purple top. In her hand she carried the hat she'd borrowed from Charity that day.

At Jameson's feet, Slim wagged his tail and whined in eager greeting. "Stay," Jameson commanded. The dog dropped to his haunches with another hopeful whimper.

"Hello, Mr. John," said Vanessa. She looked a little worried. Jameson couldn't blame her. His dad could so easily put it together that they had something going on. And not only that—the old man had spoken out against her when she won the Miss Bronco crown.

His dad whipped off his hat. "You call me Randall, you hear?" Even Jameson blinked in surprise when his dad said that. Randall sounded downright friendly. And then he glanced at Jameson and muttered, "Shut your mouth before the flies get in, son." He turned to Vanessa again. Fiddling nervously with his hat brim, he said, "My daughter gave me a talking-to about your win last Friday. She says you are the chosen Miss Bronco and I need to respect that. After giving it some thought, I have realized that my little girl is right. I want to apologize for my rude behavior at the pageant and to congratulate you on winning that crown. Also, since the day you won, I've seen you in action—at the barbecue and the rodeo—and you are doing our town proud."

Vanessa actually looked flustered. "Your daughter is very special."

"She is indeed."

"And thank you, Randall."

He donned his hat again. "Are you looking for Charity?"

"Well, yes." She gave the old man a big smile with maybe a touch of relief in it. After all, if his dad assumed that she'd come to see Charity, then she wouldn't have to answer any uncomfortable questions about what else she might be doing here. "Charity's been so great, helping me out, showing me the ropes. She lent me this hat to wear for the pet contest out at Happy Hearts, and I didn't get it back to her before she left."

"Truth is, my little girl is growing up. She's always out with her friends these days. I'm guessing she won't be home till later tonight—but I will be more than happy to give her that hat."

"Would you? Thanks."

Randall took the hat and wiggled his thick eyebrows at Jameson. "Tri-tips?"

"Thanks, Dad. Some other time."

"How about you, young lady?" Randall offered. "Care to join the John family for the best tri-tips in the county? We're also serving grilled corn on the cob and a fat baked potato slathered in butter and sour cream."

"It sounds so good and I appreciate the invitation, but I already have a date tonight."

"Ah. Another time, then?"

"I would love that."

With a quick salute, Jameson's dad turned for his pickup. He waved at them as he drove away.

"That went pretty well," said Vanessa with a careful smile. She knelt to greet Slim. "Hello, handsome. How're you doing?" Slim whimpered with happiness as she scratched his ears. "I like your dad," she said as she looked up and their eyes met.

He gave her a slow smile. "Surprised?"

"A little. I mean, he didn't seem too crazy about me last Friday."

"He can be hotheaded sometimes, but he owns

up when he blows it—and was it wishful thinking on my part, or did you call tonight a date?"

She rose. "You're cooking me dinner. Kind of feels like a date to me."

"So, we've moved on from hookup, then? We're past one-night stand?"

She gave a little snort of laughter. "How about summer romance?"

"That'll do." He wrapped an arm around her waist and pulled her close. She felt so good in his arms. "For now." Yeah, he was testing her a little. He wanted to see if she'd jump to denials and insist again that they had an agreement, that she was leaving at the end of August no matter what.

She didn't. Instead, she said, "I brought wine and brookies."

"What's a brookie?"

"Half brownie, half cookie."

"Did you bake them yourself?"

"Nope. Callie did. Trust me, you're glad about that. I burn everything I bake."

He ran a finger down the side of her throat, just to feel the texture of her soft skin. Teasingly, he asked, "But isn't baking just chemistry—and isn't science your best subject?"

She gave him an eye roll. "Hypothetically, yes. In practice, I'm thinking there's a baking gene and I don't have it. That's my excuse and let's leave it at that."

He kissed her. She tasted so good, and he let his hands stray a little, into the dip of her lower back and then out over the soft, gorgeous twin curves of her bottom. "Where are you hiding these brookies you brought?"

"Well, it's like this. I kind of freaked when I saw your dad and I left them and the wine in the car."

"You were scared he would figure out that we're a thing, you and me?"

"Yeah—and then I went and made that remark about having a date. What was I thinking? He'll say something to someone and it'll get back to my mom and grandmother."

"No worries there, and I mean that. My dad knows how to mind his own business."

"Well, good, then. I'm glad." She glanced away and then back.

"Whatever it is, just say it."

"I feel guilty, that's all. I made you promise not to tell anyone about you and me..."

"What? You think I said something to my dad? I didn't."

"No. Did you hear me? I said *I* feel guilty. Ergo, the problem is not with you."

He took both her hands and pressed them against his chest. "Vanessa. Why do you feel guilty?"

"I swore you to secrecy about you and me—

and then I told Charity that you and I will be seeing each other this summer. Callie knows, too."

"Wait. You're saying we don't have to be a secret, after all?"

Before he even had a chance to feel happy about that, she shook her head. "I'm saying I told them because they'd already pretty much figured out what was going on. Then I made them both promise to keep the information to themselves."

He tried to look on the bright side. At least he didn't have to be a secret to every single soul in Bronco—though really, he didn't get her continued insistence that no one could know. It made no sense that a strong, smart woman like her couldn't simply tell her family to back off.

But he wanted her. A lot. He'd spent all of last winter and right on through spring missing her. Something about her really got to him. She made him want to try again. And after the complete disappointment of his marriage to Maybelle, he'd had his doubts that he'd ever want to try again.

He took her hand. "Come on. Let's get the goodies from your car and I'll put the steaks on."

She pulled him back. "What's your hurry?" Her lush mouth was right there, tempting him.

What could he do but take it? He covered those soft lips with his and drank in her sweet, pleasured sigh.

Really, he could stand here on the front step kissing her forever.

But he made himself pull away. "Wine," he reminded her. "And those brownie things. We need to get those. I have to feed you."

She went up on tiptoe and stole another quick kiss. "You seem so determined."

"I am. You'll need your energy for the night to come."

Chapter Eight

Van found being with Jameson downright addictive. He said he felt the same.

They easily fell into a rhythm of spending their evenings together. That first night, Monday, she did pretty well. She climbed from his bed at two on Tuesday morning and went home to Callie's. But Tuesday night, she slept straight through until seven thirty Wednesday morning and ended up scrambling to get back to the apartment, shower and change and not end up late for Young Adventurers.

Tuesday night, she went against her own rules, taking toiletries and a change of clothes to Jameson's with her. "Just in case," she explained when she walked in his door.

He grabbed her hand, led her down the short hall to his room, and into the walk-in closet, where he'd cleared off hanger space and emptied three drawers. "Bring more stuff. Bring all your stuff. I have plenty of room."

She hung the clothes she'd brought on the empty rod and shook her head. "That's a slippery slope."

He hooked a big arm around her waist and pulled her close. After a long, steamy kiss, he nuzzled the side of her neck and argued, "When it comes to you, slippery slopes are my favorite kind. I told you. I want your nights. I want *all* the nights. All summer long." He kissed her again.

They didn't leave the closet for another hour. He had two condoms in his pocket, and to her that seemed altogether too convenient—not that she complained while he had his hands on her.

After the second go-round, when the two of them were lying on the floor of the closet on a makeshift bed of his coats, with a rolled-up pair of overalls for a pillow, she asked him about that. "Did you plan to have your way with me in this closet?"

He gave her a slow, shameless grin. "Yes, I did. In this closet—and anywhere else we happen to be. I'm not fussy. You, me and proper protection. The way I see it, that's a recipe for lasting happiness."

Before dinner, he took her out to see his prize breeding bulls and explained that he'd developed the Double J's artificial insemination program. When she wanted to know more, he led her into the office on the lower level of the house, sat her down at the PC there and gave her a virtual tour of DoubleJGenetics.com.

"We train ranchers in artificial insemination," he explained. "And the Double J provides AI services to breeders who don't want to perform the process themselves. We also sell semen. Finding the right sire is the key to the long-term health of any herd. And using semen from new bulls on a regular basis means genetic diversity and that helps keep a herd strong."

The scientist in her found the whole process spellbinding. She asked a lot of questions, each of which he answered patiently, in satisfying detail, finally teasing her, "Only you would find artificial insemination fascinating."

He started kissing her, which led to a mutually satisfying interval right there on his desk. Both of their stomachs were growling by the time he put the chicken on the grill.

After dinner, they watched a movie and then went to bed about eleven—but not to sleep. One time was never enough for either of them. And two just seemed like another reason to make love again.

Thursday morning, she was really glad she'd brought a change of clothes. She showered at Jameson's. He jumped in with her, and not really to get clean. When she finally got dressed and ready to go, it was a little after eight. She drove too fast to Happy Hearts, watching for state troopers. Her luck held. She didn't get a ticket, and she made it to Happy Hearts on time.

When she got back to the apartment that afternoon, she found Callie making herself a sandwich in the kitchen.

Callie held up a butter knife coated in mayonnaise and faked a look of alarm. "Who are you and what are you doing in my apartment?"

"Very funny."

"Don't get defensive." Callie gave her a coaxing smile. "I'm only kidding. I'm glad you're having a wonderful summer—and yes, I do consider it my job to give you a hard time."

"I get that. I mean, what are friends for?"

"Exactly. How about a chicken salad sandwich?"

"I had lunch, thanks. And you're home early."

"Evan gave me a few hours off."

"Wait. Let me guess. You have to work tonight."

"A couple of rich out-of-towners have booked a

large group. And what fun is a ghost tour in day-light? I'll be lucky to get home by midnight." She grabbed a banana from the fruit bowl, peeled it and had a bite. "So, I take it things are going well with you and Jameson?" As Van tried to decide how to respond to that, Callie teased, "Can't do without him, huh?"

"No. Yes. Maybe."

Callie pointed her bitten-off banana at Van. "I like that you always give me definitive answers."

Van scoffed at her friend's teasing and then made a sad face. "I do miss hanging out."

"Me, too."

"We need a girls' night."

"We do, yes." Callie finished off her banana and turned to dispose of the peel. "But I have to work and you're going to the Double J."

"Yeah. There is that. I just came by to grab a change of clothes. For some reason I seem inca-pable of getting out of Jameson's bed when my alarm goes off in the morning."

"Just take a suitcase. Stop making it so hard on yourself."

"I should be more…" Van let her voice trail off as she sought the right word. "Disciplined, I guess. Last New Year's, I made him promise that it was only that one night and no more. And now, here we are, having *more* because I want to be with him, and he wants to be with me. This time, I made him agree that it's only for the summer and nobody else gets to know. And then you figured out that we're seeing each other and so did Charity."

"Van. Don't. It's not wrong to be with someone you really like."

"Yeah, but I need *not* to get carried away."

"That's not true." Callie regarded her so steadily. "You're *afraid* to get carried away."

Van wanted to go straight to denial. But there was no point. Callie would see right through her. Van trusted Callie and had told her all the painful things she'd never felt ready to share with her own family. Callie knew exactly why she would never return to Bronco to live. "You're right. I *am* afraid. I feel out of control over him."

"And that scares you, to be out of control?"

"Yeah. When I really fall for someone, it never goes well. I don't seem to know how to do casual. I get all wrapped up in the guy—and then he messes me over."

"But that doesn't mean it will never go well. What's that old saying? You have to kiss a lot of frogs? I'm thinking that it's possible you've finally met your prince."

"Ugh! Don't you even." Van laughed, but it came out sounding nervous and strange. "I'm a grown woman. I don't believe in princes anymore."

"Liar."

"It's the truth, I promise you."

"Tell that to someone who doesn't know you better." Callie picked up her sandwich and took a bite.

"I can't stand here and argue the point with you. I have to get going." She turned for the hallway to the bedrooms.

"Pack a suitcase!" Callie called after her.

"You brought a suitcase." Jameson looked far too happy about that.

Just inside his door, she set the suitcase down in order to properly greet Slim, who kissed her with way too much wet, floppy tongue. "Ew. You're such an eager guy—but I'm glad to see you, too." She petted him and scratched his ears and then grabbed the suitcase and rose to her feet. "Callie insisted. What could I do?"

He pulled her close. She dropped the suitcase again as they indulged in a toe-curling, bone-melting kiss.

When he finally lifted his head, he said, "Come on. I'll help you unpack."

"Down, boy." She flattened a hand on his hard chest. "You stay out here. If you go in that walk-in closet with me, we might never come back out."

"And that's somehow a bad thing?"

She bent and grabbed the suitcase again. "I'll

be quick." He had that look, like he intended to follow her. She pointed a finger at him. "You be good." And she headed for the master bedroom.

When she emerged a few minutes later, he had a glass of wine waiting on the kitchen island for her. She cut up a salad, and he served the meatball stew he had ready on the stove.

The food was delicious. "You're a good cook," she said as she spooned up another yummy bite.

He shrugged. "My ex-wife didn't cook. One of us had to do it."

She wanted to ask about the ex. But it seemed like a bad idea to go down that road. Too serious. Too much the kind of thing people talked about when they were building a real relationship. She and Jameson weren't building anything. Uh-uh. They had fun together and it was just for the summer and she needed to keep it light. So she teased, "And here you are, spending your nights with another woman who can barely boil water."

"Lucky for you I know my way around a kitchen. It's a long drive into town just to pick up a pizza."

"Where's Grubhub when you need it, huh?"

"Exactly. I did have a cook for a while, but that didn't last. So I do it myself. And I eat at the main house a lot. It all works out."

She enjoyed a spoonful of stew and felt a little

bit guilty. "I'm monopolizing you the past few days."

His boot touched hers under the table. Even through two separate layers of rawhide and their socks, she felt that contact acutely. "It's not considered monopolizing when I want you here."

"Yeah, it is. You may be happy about it, but I'm still monopolizing you."

He toasted her with his longneck. "I'm so glad we cleared that up."

She probably shouldn't ask, but somehow the question got out anyway. "Your parents, your brothers? Have they noticed that my Subaru has been parked in front of your house every night this week?"

"I have no idea. They haven't mentioned it."

The doorbell chimed.

Now what? It occurred to her that she hadn't thought this thing through.

Spend every night with Jameson?

Yes, please! But nobody can know that we're having a thing.

All righty, then. What happens when the doorbell rings?

She had no idea, because the thought of the doorbell ringing had never so much as crossed her mind.

Jameson chuckled as he stood. "You aren't going to run and hide under my bed, are you?"

"Am I being ridiculous?"

He'd started toward the door but stopped and turned back to her with a tender, questioning look. "You know, you—" The doorbell chimed again, cutting him off. "On my way!" he shouted, then said gently to her, "I'll be right back."

She watched him cross the great room and disappear around a corner into the front hall. A moment later, she heard him talking to someone, the answering voice as deep and masculine as Jameson's own. And then she heard the door close.

Jameson reappeared—alone—and came back to her. He took his chair again. "Just Dawson dropping off a load of mineral barrels for me to fill in the morning." Grinning, he added, "And no, he didn't ask about your car in the driveway." He picked up his fork.

She groaned. "It's official. I *am* ridiculous."

Jameson set his fork down without taking a bite.

Ridiculous. The word rubbed him the wrong way, had him wondering who had made her doubt herself, made her feel less than the beautiful, brilliant, tenderhearted woman she actually was.

"No, you are not ridiculous," he answered firmly, eyes locked on hers.

She forced a laugh. "It was just an offhand remark."

He didn't think so. "You asked me if I thought you were ridiculous the night we met, the night you said would be our only night, the one that 'never happened.'" He air-quoted those last two aggravating words.

Her gaze slid away, and the corners of that lush mouth of hers turned down. "I did?"

"You did. That night, I thought it was sexy, that someone so gorgeous and smart and strong would let me have a glimpse of her shyness, her insecurity."

Again, she tried to pretend it was nothing. "This conversation has become altogether too serious."

"Vanessa. Please don't blow me off. One time *was* sexy and so damn cute. But now you've called yourself ridiculous again. I'm starting to believe that someone has made you doubt yourself."

He could see the pulse beating—too fast—beneath the silky olive skin of her throat. She gave a half shrug. "Okay, yeah. As you said, I do have insecurities. Sometimes I let them show. We struggled when I was a growing up. Money was always tight. I didn't have a lot of friends, and sometimes the richer kids made fun of me for not being thin, not having the right clothes, not looking just so."

"And that's why you don't want to live in

Bronco ever again? Bad memories from when you were a kid?"

"Essentially, yes."

He wanted to press her, to get her to tell him more about those memories, about who had made her feel less than beautiful and desirable, smart and bighearted. But he respected her reluctance. He could see that she wasn't ready to give him her secrets.

Maybe she never would be. And that hurt. The woman had gotten so far under his skin in such a short period of time. It amazed him.

It scared him, too. With Maybelle, he'd been ready to find love and settle down.

With Vanessa, it was so much more than just readiness. He wanted to be the man she needed, the man she wanted to move on to the next step with. The man she turned to in the night, *every* night. The man she stood with proudly in the bright light of day.

He wasn't that man. Yet.

But at least for now, he did own her nights. He intended to make the most of whatever time she gave him.

Rising, he rounded the end of the table and held out his hand. Warmth and hope spread through him when she displayed no hesitation to take it. And when he pulled her up, she came happily into his waiting arms.

He lowered his mouth to hers, and she opened to him. She tasted of wine, of desire and, just maybe, the promise of more. All good things—the things that came to a man willing to practice patience when the right woman finally came along.

As he lifted his head, her long, dark lashes fluttered open. He waited for her to meet his gaze directly before making his request. "Give me one thing…"

"Hmm?"

"The Night That Never Happened?"

Those dark eyes went dreamy. "It was a great night."

"Yes, it was. And I'm hoping we can agree to give that night the appreciation and respect it deserves."

"And how will we do that, exactly?"

"For starters, let's give that night a better name."

She tipped her head to the side, a tiny smile flirting at the edges of her mouth. "Such as?"

He had nothing, really. But he took a stab at it anyway. "The Night That *Did* Happen?"

"Ugh."

"Okay, fine," he admitted. "That's not my best work."

"True." She fiddled with the top snap on his shirt. "How about Best One-Night Stand in the

History of All the One-Night Stands Forever and Ever?"

"I love it. But it might be a tad long. Also, it's seven months later and here you are in my arms. Our first night is disqualified as a one-night stand."

"A Hookup to Remember?"

He scoffed. "Now you're insulting the wonder that is us."

"Best New Year's Eve Ever?" She popped that top snap. "Our First Night?" The second snap gave way. She pressed her lips to the slice of bare chest she'd revealed. "The Night We Could Never Forget?" She popped two more snaps as she rattled that off.

He tipped up her chin and kissed her again—a deeper, hungrier kiss than the one before.

When she dropped back to her heels, she pretended to sulk. "You are ruining my concentration. My brain doesn't work when you kiss me like that."

He bent just long enough to scoop her high in his arms. "It's okay. Right now, let's skip the thinking and get down to the action."

She laughed and grabbed him around the neck. "Wait a minute. We should clear the table first. I'll do it—after all, you cooked."

He eased her feet to the floor. "Let me help." He swept out an arm. Dishes, spoons and glassware crashed to the floor. Slim, snoozing by the fireplace, let out a whine of surprise, followed by a giant yawn.

"Jameson!" Vanessa shrieked as he scooped her up again. "I can't believe you just did that."

"Yeah?" He growled the words against the velvety skin of her throat as he lowered her to the just cleared table. "Wait'll you see what I do next."

She sighed as he kissed her. And then she moaned. And before he finished making dessert of her, she screamed his name over and over again.

That weekend, he took her away—not too far. Just to a family-owned cabin in the mountains a few miles from town. They picnicked in the wildflowers of his favorite secluded meadow and swam buck naked in the icy creek formed by a hidden underground spring.

Saturday night in bed after a couple of satisfying bouts of enthusiastic lovemaking, she stacked her hands on his bare chest and closed her eyes. "I could lie here like this forever."

He combed her hair back from her temples with his fingers, catching a random swatch of the thick, silky stuff and slowly wrapping it around his hand. "Don't get too comfortable. I'm edging up on feeling frisky again."

With a big, fake groan, she rolled off him and snuggled up to his side. "You are insatiable."

"Are you complaining?"

"No way."

"That's what I wanted to hear." He ran his palm up the velvety skin of her back and fiddled with her gorgeous, wildly tangled hair some more. "One more time with you always seems like a great idea. But a gentleman never wears out his welcome."

She reached up, touched the side of his face in a tender, slow caress. Her fingertips skimmed his short beard, skated higher to brush his bare cheek.

He pulled her close enough to kiss the end of her nose. "You seem thoughtful."

"Well, I want to ask you something, but maybe it's too personal…"

He caught those fingers, brought them to his lips and bit the tips, lightly. "Nothing you could ask would be too personal. Go for it."

"You said you were married…?"

Damn. Finally.

He'd been waiting for her to ask about Maybelle. Not so much because he looked forward to telling her what a fool he'd been, but because he wanted to get closer to her. And he'd learned enough from past experience to know that to get closer, a guy had to open up. He had to show a woman the things he was proud of—and the stuff he could have handled a whole lot better.

"Her name was Maybelle. Maybelle Butler."

Vanessa frowned. "Her name's familiar. Should I know of her?"

"Most likely. She's a rodeo queen, a champion barrel racer."

Vanessa drew in a sharp breath. "Petite, right? Acres of red hair? And really pretty?"

"That's Maybelle. Beyond being a star, she's also a fine horse trainer. Six years ago, at the end of the rodeo season, she showed up at the Double J looking for a winter job to tide her over. My dad hired her on the spot to work with the horses. He liked her. Maybelle's a charmer. And he was a little starstruck, that *the* Maybelle Butler had come to work for us. At his insistence, she took the foreman's cottage not far from the main house. It was empty at the time. My mom liked her, too, and extended an open invitation to dinner with the family."

"And what about you?" Vanessa asked that with a playful smile. "Let me guess. After Maybelle started working here, you spent a lot of time at the stables?"

"I did. And I went to dinner at the main house just about every night, because Maybelle did, too. What I didn't know at the time was that Maybelle had had enough of eating dust. She wanted a rancher with a decent-size bank account. She wanted a chance to take things easy, live the good life. She admitted later, when it all fell apart with her and me, that she'd set her sights on me before she showed up on the Double J asking for work."

"Wait. She went looking for a rich husband and decided you were it?"

"Yeah, but you make it sound so pretty calculated."

"Jameson," she chided. "It *is* pretty calculated."

He gave it up. "You're right. But you'd have to know Maybelle. She hadn't had an easy time of it. She'd been raised in the Bronco area, on a few acres of dry grass and scrub brush ten miles from town—what some would generously call a ranchette."

"So then, she knew all about you and she'd shown up looking for a job in order to get close to you, in particular. You're saying that it wasn't just any rich guy she wanted. She'd set her sights on you."

"That's right. She was open about that with me from the start. She said she'd had a crush on me back in high school."

"You were flattered."

"You bet I was."

"Did you remember her from high school?"

"No."

"Because you hung out with the Taylors and

the Abernathys and the other rich kids on the big ranches and in Bronco Heights."

He tugged on the lock of hair he'd wrapped around his finger. "Is that an accusation?"

"Maybe. A little. I was a poor girl, too. I sympathize with a girl like Maybelle. And please continue with the story. I'm through busting your chops just because you're a rich guy—for now, anyway. Tell me more about Maybelle."

"When she was seventeen, she ran away from home in the middle of the night driving the ancient pickup she'd bought from a junkyard and sweet-talked her mechanic boyfriend into fixing up. From her hard-drinking daddy, she stole a horse trailer and the only thing at that run-down ranchette that she loved, a pretty little paint named Fancy Lady."

"She ran away to ride the rodeo circuit?"

"Yes, she did."

Vanessa made a sound of approval low in her throat. "Maybelle sounds like a fighter. I like that."

And I like you, he thought. *So much. Maybe more than is good for me.*

Twin lines formed between Vanessa's smooth, dark brows. "Jameson, you look worried suddenly. What's the matter?"

He shook his head and lied. "Not a thing—and yeah. Maybelle's a fighter, and I liked that, too."

Vanessa watched his face so closely. "You fell hard."

"I did. Looking back, I can see all the ways she and I weren't a good fit. At the time though, I wanted her enough to tell myself it was true. Essentially, I was ready to settle down, get married, raise a family. Maybelle said she wanted a family, too. So we tied the knot. I thought I had it all."

"What went wrong?"

"She'd lied about what she really wanted, but not maliciously. I think, first and foremost, she'd lied to herself. Looking back now, I think that pretty soon after the wedding, she began to realize that being a rancher's wife didn't work for her, after all."

"She told you this?"

"Not till much later. Not till the end. She'd thought she wanted a settled-down life, but then she missed the action, the variety of the rodeo circuit. She craved excitement, and she wasn't getting it living with me on the Double J."

"Then why didn't she just start entering rodeos again? Why couldn't she be a rodeo star and your wife, too?"

"It's a good question. If she'd faced the problem early on and told me about it, maybe we could have worked it out. But in hindsight, I would say her pride wouldn't let her do that. She'd really come on strong about hating the rodeo life, being sick and tired of living from one win to the next, wanting to make a home, have a family. Before we got married, she insisted that she wanted to start trying for a baby right away."

"And you…?"

"I agreed."

"Because of what you said at New Year's, right? That you want kids, the whole family thing."

"Right. But somehow, time went by and Maybelle never got pregnant."

"How much time?"

"Three years."

"Did you guys see a doctor, find out what the problem might be?"

"After we were married a year and a half or so, I suggested that. She put me off. She said everything would be fine. We just needed more time, she would get pregnant eventually, we would have the family we'd planned for. I didn't push. I'm not sure why. I think I was also having second thoughts about our marriage, second thoughts I didn't want to admit to, not even to myself. I should have been more focused on what was really going on between the two of us. That should've come first. But instead, I was all about 'making a family,' as though having kids is how you build a relationship.

"It wasn't really working between Maybelle

and me and I think, somewhere in the back of my mind, I did finally start realizing that having a baby when everything felt so up in the air wouldn't be a solution to anything. Maybelle and me, we weren't big on communication. We were drifting apart, and I knew it and I let it happen."

Vanessa laid her hand on the side of his face. "I'm so sorry, Jameson."

He turned his mouth into her hand, breathed a kiss in the heart of her palm. "I didn't fight for her, for what we had. Somehow, by the time a couple of years had passed, whatever connection we'd shared at first was pretty much gone—and then, near the end of the third year, I found the discarded packaging from her birth control pills."

Vanessa's eyes got extra wide. "Wow."

"Yeah. That's when I finally decided to talk to her about it."

"Well, that's good, that you two started talking, right?"

"It should've been, but I was pissed—more than pissed. I was furious. I demanded to know how long she'd been on the pill. She gave my attitude right back to me, said a better question would be when had she ever been *off* the pill, because she hadn't."

"Omigod."

"Yeah. It was bad. I was mad enough to spit nails, and even though I'd also had second thoughts about her and me, about rushing toward parenthood rather than figuring out how to live and work together as a couple, I didn't admit any of that. I made no effort to try to talk to her honestly about it. I went straight to an ultimatum. I ordered her to throw her pills away immediately, or it was over between us. And she said, 'Fine. Have it your way, then. I want a divorce.'"

"Oh, Jameson..." Vanessa cuddled in close. Tucking her head under his chin, she pressed her lips to the side of his throat. "How awful. I truly am so, so sorry..." The words were warm and comforting, like her breath against his skin.

He stroked her hair, then caught her earlobe between his thumb and finger and rubbed it gently. "Yeah, it was a bad moment. I was an ass. Maybelle was scrappy as ever." Looking back now, after the anger and the emptiness that followed, after the divorce and the slow realization that he and Maybelle never really had a chance, he could almost smile at the memory. "She said it was just as well I found out that she'd never stopped taking her pills. Said she couldn't go on living this boring life, said that yeah, she was still kind of crazy about me, but being a ranch wife? Not for her. She told me straight out, 'Jameson, I need this marriage to be over or I will start to hate you, and there's no good in that.'"

"So...?"

"So, it was more than apparent to both of us by then that the marriage *was* over—that it was pretty much doomed right out of the gate. She'd lied to me. Looking back, I get why she wasn't real big on open, honest communication. She'd spent her whole life fighting to make her own way and she had no communication skills whatsoever. Frankly, I was no better. I was a bad husband to her, a guy who never made the effort to find out what was going on with her until it was way too late. I gave her the divorce. We agreed on a one-time settlement. I paid her off, and that was that."

"How long ago did all this happen?"

"She moved out two years ago. Haven't seen her since."

Vanessa tipped her head back. Those dark eyes gleamed at him. Sometimes when she looked at him, he felt she could see inside his head.

Finally, she spoke again. "You don't seem bitter."

"I'm past all that, but I was plenty bitter at first. I told myself I hated her. I thought she'd played me good and proper. And she did. But over time, I started to admit to myself that it takes two to make a marriage—a good one *or* one that fails."

"Hmm." Vanessa held his gaze. "I don't know that she played you, really. It sounds like Maybelle played herself. You were collateral damage."

"Ouch."

"What? You'd prefer to think that she played you on purpose, that she used you and took advantage of your trust?"

He laughed then. "Yeah, I would."

She tucked her head down again and muttered something about men under her breath. He decided not to ask what.

"Hey." He curled a finger under her chin, lifting her face up so that she looked at him. Once she focused those fine eyes on him, he rubbed his thumb back and forth across her pillowy mouth. "You're tough on a guy, you know that, Miss Bronco?"

"Just calling it the way I see it."

He rolled to his back and pulled her with him, so all that lush softness ended up on top of him, tempting him. He wanted her again. But then, he always did.

She asked, "You really think I'm too tough on you?"

Gruffly, he commanded, "Kiss me," and lifted his head to capture her lips.

She pulled back to grin down at him. "You didn't answer my question."

"All right. You're a *little* too tough on me, maybe."

"Aww. Poor baby."

"No guy likes to think of himself as collateral

damage, like he's just an incidental bad result from a woman working through her problems."

"I hear you. But, Jameson, isn't it always that way when love doesn't work out? For both people, really? They've been writing songs about collateral damage forever. From 'You Always Hurt the One You Love' and onward. People hurt each other because they're too busy struggling through their own crap to be careful of the other person's heart. To me, that seems better somehow, than to mess someone over on purpose. At the end, Maybelle said she was still 'kind of crazy' about you. That means she really did love you. She just wasn't very good at loving."

"Maybelle being 'kind of crazy' about me is not anything that I would call love."

"I only mean she still cared about you. The way you just told it to me, even at the end she seemed to have real affection for you. That's something, isn't it? That matters."

"Yeah, I guess so."

"But you're not sure?"

"Who can say? Whether she played me or I was just random damage of her acting out her own personal drama, it didn't work out. I felt really bad for a while. But I'm over it now." He eased his fingers up under the heavy fall of her hair and wrapped them around her nape. "Right now, I want you to kiss me. A kiss would make everything so much better."

"How, exactly, is a kiss going to fix anything?"

"Trust me. It will."

"A woman knows not to trust a guy who says, 'trust me.'"

"Do it anyway." He guided her head down so that their lips almost touched. "Make my night. Your kiss is the solution to all the world's problems."

"Oh, you are a silver-tongued devil, Jameson John."

"Kiss me, Vanessa."

On a sweet little sigh, she covered his waiting mouth with hers. He wrapped his arms tighter around her and wished for things he would probably never have.

Chapter Nine

After that night at the cabin, the night Jameson opened up to her about his marriage to Maybelle Butler, Van stopped trying to tell herself she needed to pull away. She gave up feeling guilty for not maintaining a certain emotional distance from him.

His honesty about what had happened in his marriage had gotten to her, weakened her resolve not to let him too close. She fully accepted now that, if he'd once been a player, those days were gone. Though she continued to insist that they not go public in Bronco, she gave herself up to spending every moment she could with him.

The next weekend, they made the two-and-a-half-hour drive to Bozeman and stayed at the Armory Hotel in a beautiful, restful suite with a king-size bed and sheets so soft she hated to get out of bed in the morning. In Bozeman, they did all the touristy things. They hiked the Bridger Foothills National Scenic Trail, visited the Museum of the Rockies and the American Computer and Robotics Museum.

Hand in hand, they strolled Main Street downtown, stopping to window-shop and so she could pick up a couple of souvenirs. It was so good, just to be with him out in the open without worrying that someone might see them together and say something to her mom or Grandma Daisy.

Getting away alone, just the two of them, had her giving more thought to her own insistence on secrecy. Van started to see that her fear didn't really center on her family. She would never move home just because they pressured her to.

The problem lay in her own vulnerable, hopeful heart. Once she outed her relationship with Jameson in her hometown, she would become so much more likely to let herself go further, to start imagining a future with him, to long for a real, lasting bond with him.

That way lay trouble. Tempting, lovely trouble—but trouble, nonetheless.

To give her trust again, take a chance on love again…

No.

The risk still felt greater than the possible rewards. To give in, let herself fall and believe that he would be there to catch her…

It was asking too much of her battered heart.

As the second week of July became the third and she spent every moment she could steal at Jameson's side, Van somehow managed to cling to their original agreement—that it was only for the summer, that at the end of August she *would* walk away.

So what that the pull between them only seemed to get stronger? So what that she loved being with him, in bed and out?

So what that sometimes she could almost picture a life with him, right here in Bronco, close to her family?

She had her life all worked out, and love would not mess with it. Not this time. She'd been hurt once too often. No way was she headed for heartbreak again.

The weekend after their Bozeman getaway, Van and Jameson decided to stick close to the ranch. Saturday morning, she woke with his arms around her and knew she wouldn't be heading for Happy Hearts to have coffee with Daphne and

Evan, wouldn't be there later to help with whatever chores needed doing.

She felt a little bit guilty about that...

But not guilty enough to leave the warm shelter of Jameson's arms.

"Mornin'." His voice was sleep-rough and arousing, as was the feel of his warm palm skating over the curve of her hip and easing inward in search of all her womanly secrets.

She gave them all up to him. Twice. Once with his face buried between her thighs as he coaxed a powerful orgasm from her using his clever mouth and thrillingly rough, hardworking hands. And then, a few minutes later, she surrendered again, this time with him buried deep inside her, rising with her to the top of the world, soaring over the edge into free fall only seconds after she did.

For a while, as the sun rose and sent fingers of golden light easing in around the edges of the blinds, they just lay there together. She felt so close to him, happy and unguarded, completely content.

Which might have been the reason why, later, after breakfast, when they sat at the long table in his kitchen together, relaxing over that second cup of coffee, she failed to evade when he said, "Sometimes lately, like this morning, I get the feeling you're learning to trust me at least a little."

"I do trust you," she answered softly with a

smile to match. "You're a good man, Jameson, you really are."

He gazed at her so steadily as he offered his hand. She took it. They wove their fingers together across the tabletop.

"What is it, then?" he asked. "What happened to you? I know you joke about the players who did you wrong. And I'm sorry for all that. But there's something else, something deeper, I think. Something that happened right here, in Bronco. Something that you can never quite get past, never completely forgive."

She didn't look away. "You're right. My worst heartbreak happened here."

"Will you tell me about it?" He said it so gently, not expecting her to give him her hardest truth, but asking her to share if she might be willing.

That he'd asked so quietly, so hopefully—it mattered. She couldn't deny those deep blue eyes, couldn't refuse him the answer he sought.

She did pull her hand from his, though. She retreated to her side of the table, withdrawing from him, surrendering to her instinct for self-protection. "You would have to promise not to do anything about what I tell you—not to try to track down the people involved. I need your word that you will just leave it alone."

"The people involved?" He kept his voice

carefully controlled—but not carefully enough. "What the hell happened, Vanessa?"

"That." She pointed at him. "Right there. You can't do that. You can't protect me from something that happened years ago, something I've dealt with in my own way. If I tell you this story, you have to let it be."

"I can't promise you—"

"If you can't agree to let it go after I tell you, then I won't tell you." He just glared at her until she prompted, "Yes or no, Jameson? Will you keep my confidence about this or not?"

"Damn it, Vanessa."

"Yes or no?"

He blew out a hard breath. "All right. Yes, I'll keep your confidence. You have my word."

She rose and poured herself yet another cup of coffee. When she held out the pot, he nodded. Once she'd topped him off and put the pot back, she took her seat again.

How to even begin? "When I was thirteen, I fell in love with my best friend..."

Taking care not to use any names, she told him about her love for Donnie Bell. Jameson sat there, barely moving, his gaze holding hers, as she spoke.

"I believed," she said, "I really did, that he and I were forever. That nothing could rip us apart..."

Jameson listened, eyes locked on her, never

once glancing away, as she told him everything, how the boy she loved betrayed her for a prettier, more popular girl, a girl with a rich dad who could offer him a better future. She told how Donnie came back to her—for one night—and then betrayed her all over again the next day.

"The new girlfriend and *her* friends, they were brutal. They called me a lot of ugly names, said I was a cheat and a man stealer, a lowlife, a loser and, well, you know—all the awful words they use on girls sometimes. They tripped me in the halls, scrawled really disgusting things on my locker, even broke into it, tore up my stuff and then lit it all on fire."

He asked why the school hadn't done something.

"Nobody talked and nobody got caught. I knew who did what—they made sure that I knew—but that doesn't mean I could prove anything."

"What about the guy?" demanded Jameson, his eyes hard now, angry, a muscle ticking in his jaw. "Seems to me like he was the lowlife."

"Jameson." She adjusted her black-framed glasses on the bridge of her nose. "It was high school. I was an idiot to go back for more with him, to believe him when he swore he'd made a big mistake and he would never, ever hurt me again. I should have learned my lesson about him when he dumped me the first time."

"Just give me that douchebag's name."

Had she known that was coming? Yeah. "Not going to happen. You gave me your word that you would stay out of it."

"Who else knows about this?"

"A few of my closest girlfriends, a therapist I saw a few years later—and now you. Other than that, no one."

"What about your mother, your grandmother, your brother?"

"No way. Evan would have hit the roof and gone after my old boyfriend just the same as you want to do right now."

"A man needs to protect the people he—"

"Stop. Look, my family knew it hadn't worked out with that boy and that I was heartbroken over it. But that's all they knew. It was my battle. I fought it. And it's long over now."

"It's not over if you won't ever even consider living in Bronco again because of what happened back then."

"Stop. I mean it. You're just proving to me why I never should have told you a thing."

Silence. A bleak one. They scowled at each other across the suddenly yawning span of the tabletop.

Finally, his expression softened. He asked gently, with care, with respect, "Tell me the rest?"

"Not if you're going to go all caveman on me."

"You're right. I gave my word, and I will stick by it. I'll keep my shit together."

She probably shouldn't tell him. What good would it do, really, to share her ultimate teenage humiliation with him?

But she really did care for him so much now. She wanted him to understand why she was who she was, why she could only go so far with him. "You know Digger's Trail?" In densely wooded wilderness a few miles from town, Digger's Trail wound upward into the mountains.

"Yeah, I know it."

"I used to go there to get away by myself, when things were rough, when I needed to be alone. Before we broke up, I would go with the boy who dumped me. Anyway, a few weeks before high school graduation, those girls who were bullying me, they followed me up there…"

Even nine years later, it made her heart beat a lurching rhythm in her chest, caused sweat to break out on her upper lip, to remember it, the way they'd surrounded her, slapped at her, mocked her, called her all the usual hideous, cruel names.

"They had a rope. They overpowered me and tied me to a tree. They put a burlap sack over my head and left me there."

"My God. For how long?"

"A few hours. Eventually, a couple of tourists found me."

"Tell me you went to the sheriff."

"No, I did not. The tourists tried to talk me into reporting the incident. I refused. I thanked them. I said I was fine, and I went home."

"Fine? You weren't fine."

"No, I wasn't. But that's what I did, the choice that I made at the time. I was eighteen and I had my pride, and I decided to handle it myself."

"How badly were you injured?"

"Not at all—not physically, anyway. All they did was slap me around and back me into the tree so that one of them could throw the rope around me and they could tie me up."

"It was still an assault."

"Yeah. But I'll say it again. I did what I did, and it was a long time ago."

"But you did retaliate?"

She nodded. "That night, I broke into the school, jimmied open their lockers, tore up what was inside them and poured pancake syrup on what I'd already ripped to pieces. Nobody caught me, and I felt vindicated."

"And then what?"

"And that's all. Believe it or not, after that, it was over. Those girls never bothered me again and the boy stayed clear of me. Looking back,

I think maybe those girls actually scared themselves with what they did to me on Digger's Trail."

"You could have been attacked by a cougar or a bear. You could've—"

"I know. And after that, I was angry for a long time. Nobody messed with me. Everyone left me alone, and I was fine with that. I was through with Bronco High and the boy who broke my heart and those mean girls and everything else about this town. I left for college in the fall, and I moved to Billings as soon as I graduated. I've lived there ever since."

He got up, circled the table and went to stand above her. "Come up here. Please." He held out his hand.

She eyed it cautiously, but then finally put her fingers in his. He pulled her up and into his arms. With a sigh, she leaned into his solid strength. "I did get therapy. I worked through it. I really am okay."

He held her a little closer. She felt his lips brush the crown of her head. "You're a fighter, that's for sure."

She looked up at him then. "And believe it or not, the experience has helped me as a teacher. I'm pretty sensitive to what goes on with my students. If someone's being bullied, I usually pick up on it and I take the necessary steps to make it stop. I make sure the offender is dealt with and the victim gets help."

"That's good."

"I think so."

"That old boyfriend of yours still needs his ass whupped, though."

"Not by you, he doesn't."

"I need to ask…"

Something in his voice sent a shiver racing down her spine. "What?"

"The guy who messed you over. Was that Don Bell?"

She gaped up at him, feeling panicked and also immobilized.

And he *knew*. "All right, then. Don was the guy and his wife, Maura, she was the ringleader of those girls who attacked you on Digger's Trail."

Van managed one word. "How…?"

He gazed down at her for the longest time before he answered. "At the barbecue on the Fourth of July, I saw you talking to them. You looked like you couldn't wait to get away."

She held his gaze, and she drilled her point home. "I mean it, Jameson. You gave me your word. Do not go after Donnie—or Maura, for that matter."

"You don't have to worry. I keep my promises. Besides…"

She wasn't sure she liked the look in his eyes. "Besides what?"

"I wouldn't have a clue what to do about Maura. I don't beat up women, and I'm guessing the statute of limitations has run out on what she did to you. As for Don Bell, I saw his face when he looked at you. He knows what he lost. I'm thinking that's payback enough for that sucker."

She was the one gaping now.

Because she believed him.

And not only about what he *wouldn't* do to Donnie Bell.

She believed in his good heart and his kind ways. She believed that he cared for her, that his word meant something to him, and he would always keep it, that he would never thoughtlessly hurt her.

She loved being with him, in bed and out. Lately, when she didn't keep a good rein on herself, she could almost picture a life with him, right here in Bronco, close to her family.

But she had to remember that was only a fantasy and fantasies ended in pain when things went bad. She just wasn't ready go there again. One way or another, it never worked out.

She only needed to hold on to reality. To enjoy this time they had together. And, when the end of summer came, to do what she'd promised to do—walk away.

Chapter Ten

Gently, Jameson eased Vanessa's glasses off and set them on the table. Then he kissed her.

The kiss heated up fast. They ended up in the bedroom once more, naked on the tangled sheets of his bed, holding on tight to each other in a bright pool of morning sun.

After the lovemaking, she closed her eyes.

He held her in his arms as she slept. She looked so peaceful. He stared down at her beautiful, freckled face, and the truth hit him like a damn wrecking ball, square in the chest.

He was in big trouble with her. He loved her.

And she'd been hurt one too many times.

She'd made it way too clear. No matter what he did to try to get through to her, she wouldn't let it happen for them. She would leave as she'd always said she would, head back to Billings at summer's end.

Maybe if he moved to Billings…

He couldn't believe he'd actually let himself consider such a thing. He'd always been a Bronco man through and through.

But sometimes a man had to prioritize, be willing to make changes to get what he wanted most. He could buy good land up there. It was only a couple of hours away from Bronco, and he could come home often, help out here when needed— and run the family AI business from the new place.

A cynical voice in his head mocked, *It doesn't matter what you do. She's not up for forever, fool.*

He knew it in his heart. She liked what they had right now, liked getting close, but with a definite end date.

Lovewise, in her life, the hits had just kept coming. She didn't have it in her to give love another chance.

He knew it. He *got* it. And still, he couldn't stop himself from hoping that somehow the two of them might make love work.

* * *

Through the layers of sleep, Van heard her cell ring.

She blinked and opened her eyes to see Jameson smiling down at her. "Sorry. I drifted off."

"No problem. That's what weekends are for." He grabbed her phone off the nightstand and gave it her.

"Thanks." The display, a little blurry without her glasses, said Mom. She put the phone to her ear. "Hey."

"Hello, honey. You sound sleepy. Did I wake you?"

"I stretched out just for a minute. Guess I must've dropped off."

"You're always on the go. You deserve a nap now and then."

Still canted up on an elbow above her, Jameson gave her a teasing smile.

With a playful nudge, she pushed him back to his own pillow. He settled on his side facing her and shut his eyes—apparently stealing a catnap while she talked to her mom.

Wanda asked about Happy Hearts and how the summer camp was going.

"Really well. We're on the reptile unit now. Everyone loves the snakes and lizards."

"Oh, I'm sure they do," said her mom. "You're a marvel with those kids."

"I do have fun with them. Most of them are still at that age where the natural world is fascinating and new. Chemical reactions give them a big thrill, and they get all excited just spotting a lizard sunning on a rock. How's everything at home?"

"All good."

"G-G?"

"Amazing as usual."

"And her new fortune-telling business?"

"Bite your tongue," Wanda chided. "Your great-grandmother does not tell fortunes. She dispenses wisdom. She claims her connections to the paranormal world are real and based on solid science and that her knowledge of human nature goes much deeper than mere fortune telling."

Van laughed. "G-G will always defend her pseudoscience to the death."

"Do *not* use the word *pseudoscience* in your great-grandmother's presence."

"Yes, Mother."

"And, honey, I was wondering…"

"Hmm?"

"The summer is flying by. I know you're busy, but we don't see you enough."

Guilt took a serious poke at her. She hadn't seen her mom, Grandma Daisy or G-G since the barbecue on the Fourth. How was that possible?

Almost three weeks had slipped by during which she'd spent every spare moment with Jameson.

She needed to get a grip on herself. Half the reason she'd let Daphne talk her into teaching the Young Adventurers for the summer was the opportunity it would give her to spend more time with her family.

Sitting up, Van pulled the sheet with her to cover her breasts as Jameson sat up and poked a thumb back over his shoulder, indicating that he would leave her to her conversation. She gave him a nod. He rolled off the bed and reached for his jeans.

"You're right, Mom. I miss you guys."

"Come to dinner tonight."

She slid a glance at Jameson. He was watching her, frowning a little as he zipped up his Wranglers. He mouthed the words, "Everything okay?"

Was it? Not really. She'd been ignoring her family to spend all her time with him. That had to stop. But she gave him another nod anyway. He turned to go. When he opened the bedroom door, Slim sat waiting on the other side. The dog gave a loud whine.

"That sounds like a dog," said her mother, as Jameson went out, silently pulling the door shut behind him. "Are you at Callie's?"

Van lied by sidestepping the question. "Dinner, huh? Sure. What time?"

"Oh, honey. That's great. Six?"

"I will be there."

"Bring Callie…" Wanda's voice trailed off and then she added kind of coyly, "Or *another* friend, if you'd like."

Van cringed. Bringing Jameson to dinner on West Street? Not going to happen. That would mean way too many questions she didn't feel like answering. Plus, it would give Jameson the wrong sort of signal—the kind of signal that didn't fit their agreement to spend time together privately, with no one else the wiser. "Thanks, Mom. I'll see you then."

"Wonderful."

They said goodbye.

For a minute or two, Van just sat there, clutching her phone against her chest, staring blindly out the slider that led to a sunlit deck. She felt out of sorts, apprehensive—but why?

Because she couldn't just lie around in Jameson's bed forever, she decided. She needed to stop gazing at nothing and get moving.

Tossing back the covers, she put on her clothes and straightened the bed.

In the kitchen, she found Jameson shutting the dishwasher door after loading in the breakfast dishes. She grabbed her glasses off the freshly wiped table, put them on and then knelt to give Slim a little love.

When she rose, Jameson came to her. He framed her face in his big hands and brushed a kiss on her forehead, just above the bridge of her glasses. "How's your mom?"

"Good, thanks."

"Everything okay with the family?"

"Fine, yes."

He guided a thick swatch of her hair back over her shoulder. "It's a warm day. How about we tack up a couple of horses? I'll show you a pretty, private spot I know right here on the Double J. It's up in the foothills, a little swimming hole. Deep enough for diving with a nice, grassy bank at water's edge to spread a blanket on."

She thought of her real life, of the family she'd essentially been ignoring, of all the ways she'd grown too attached to this beautiful man, of what she'd just revealed to him back there in his bed.

Her family didn't even know about all that. The ones who did know were women—women she trust. She'd never told anyone else. Especially not the men she'd believed herself in love with— not David or Chaz or even open-minded, mild-tempered Trevor.

Only Jameson...

Really, she needed to put a check on herself. She'd said she would go to dinner at her Mom's tonight. And she wasn't about to bring a date.

She needed to pull back a bit, get herself

some space, stop neglecting the people she cared about—the ones who would be there for her at the end of the summer when this thing with him came to its natural end.

Jameson asked gently, "What is it? What's wrong?"

"Well, I was just thinking that I've got a million things to do at Callie's. And then my mom asked me over for dinner tonight. I haven't seen the family for weeks, so of course I said yes. I would love to see that swimming hole. But really, I think I ought to pull myself together and get going."

He seemed to be studying her, but when he spoke, his tone was mild. "Of course. It's important to spend time with the family."

"Exactly."

"I'll get some work done around here today and take my own advice, join the folks for dinner at the main house."

"They probably wonder where you've been the past three weeks."

He had that thoughtful look again as he asked, "Later tonight, then?"

She felt this tug, like a hungry little ache in the vicinity of her heart, as though a strong, secret thread held her bound to him, a thread that pulled her toward him. She wanted tonight with him. She wanted *all* the nights with him. "Yes—I mean, if that's okay?"

"It's more than okay." He touched her cheek, a slow, light caress. Her nerve endings heated and fired in response. "What time?"

"Nineish?"

"I'll be here."

"Okay, then. I'll just grab my stuff and get going."

Fifteen minutes later, Vanessa came out of the bedroom with her suitcase.

Jameson played it easy and cool, though he had a bad feeling about this. She seemed withdrawn. He worried that she'd find some reason not to keep her date with him tonight.

But then he reminded himself that they both needed to pay attention to the other people in their lives. He had work he'd been putting off in order to spend more time with her.

Today, he'd get stuff done, burn ditches, check fence lines, move ornery cattle to fresh pastures. And tonight—unless she freaked and didn't show—he would find his reward in her arms.

He kissed her at the door, took comfort in the way her body pressed, warm and willing, against him. After her SUV disappeared down the ranch road, he went back inside to change into work clothes.

In the closet, he saw that she'd taken all her clothes with her.

Not a good sign.

They needed to talk—about changing the rules. About taking the next step.

Too bad he had no idea how to broach that loaded subject with her. At least he still had weeks left of summer to find a way to convince her that they could have it all if she'd only give them a half a chance.

When Van let herself into the apartment, Callie wasn't there. She gave her roomie a call.

"Honey, I'm home," she teased when Callie answered.

"Who is this?" Callie razzed her back. "How did you get this number?"

They laughed together and Van said, "I tore myself away from my sexy secret cowboy lover." She put on a sad voice. "But you're not here and I'm all alone."

"Yeah, I'm working till four."

"What about dinner? I'm going to Mom's and you're invited."

"I would love that."

By four thirty, when Callie got home, Van had done laundry, cleaned the apartment top to bottom, showered and changed.

Callie took one look at her and asked, "What's wrong?"

"It's just…" She hardly knew where to start.

"When your voice trails off like that, there's only one thing to do. Have a glass of wine with me and tell me everything."

Callie poured the wine. They sat on the sofa and Van cried on her friend's shoulder because her fun summer romance had grown way too important to her.

When she finally fell silent, Callie asked, "What exactly are you telling me? Does he want to break it off?"

"No. Not at all. He'd have me there with him 24/7 if possible."

"So then, this is a problem, because…?"

"I'm getting way too attached. It's dangerous for me to get attached. When I get attached, something always goes wrong."

Callie made prayer hands. "This could be the time it *doesn't* go wrong. Have you thought about that?"

Van tipped her head back with a groan. "You shouldn't put up with me. You're the best friend ever, way too wonderful and patient with me. I know you're right. I do." She tapped at her temple. "In here. It's just, well…"

"Love has not been kind to you. I get that. Come here." Callie reached out.

Van sank into a much-needed hug. "Thank you," she said when they broke apart.

"For what? I didn't do anything."

"For being here, being my friend."

"I just wish I could convince you that sometimes things actually do work out."

"I hear you." A change of subject was definitely in order. "Let's talk about you. How are things at Bronco Ghost Tours?"

They spent a half hour catching up and left for the house on West Street early.

The whole family was there—including Evan and Daphne. Van took pleasure in watching her mom and Sean together. Her mom seemed genuinely happy with Sean—as happy as Evan was with Daphne. Grandma Daisy talked about the series of watercolors she was working on, and G-G demanded that they all pay her a visit at Wisdom by Winona.

Van loved them all a lot, and she enjoyed the evening.

Except…

Thoughts of Jameson kept intruding. A day away from him and she couldn't wait to throw herself into his arms again. She needed to get a grip on herself, chill a little when it came to him. She needed to give more time to her real life.

For instance, tomorrow. She ought to head over to Happy Hearts early, have coffee with Daphne and Evan, hang around to help muck out some stalls, gather and prep the necessary materials for upcoming projects at Young Adventurers.

Really, she needed to leave the Double J in time to sleep in her own bed for a change. Using Jameson's house as her home base had to stop.

When he heard Vanessa's SUV pull up to the house at nine that evening, relief washed over Jameson, cool and soothing as a dip in a cold creek on a blistering summer day. He'd started to worry she wouldn't show.

But he opened the door, and she ran to his arms. He kissed her hard and deep—and took her straight to bed.

Later, he got them each a longneck and they drank them right there in bed. She laughed at his story about Slim tangling with a garter snake that bit him on the nose and wouldn't let go. He asked about her family, and she said everyone was fine.

They started kissing again and that led to more lovemaking. Around midnight, she fell asleep in his arms.

He woke sometime later, alone in the bed. "Vanessa?"

No answer. The bathroom door was wide open, with nothing but darkness inside. He got up and pulled on his Wranglers. With Slim at his heels, he went out into the main room.

No sign of Vanessa. He didn't really have to check the driveway for her Forester to know she was gone. But he checked it anyway.

He stood on the front step staring at the empty driveway. At his feet, Slim gave a sad little whine. He looked down into those big, soulful brown eyes. "It appears she took off, buddy."

Back in his room, he sent Slim to his bed in the corner and picked up his phone. No voice mail, no text. He started to call her. But come on, what would he say? Would he end up begging?

Vanessa, please. Talk to me. Tell me what's wrong.

No.

He needed to wait for the right moment to get into it with her. Two o'clock on Sunday morning wasn't it. He let it go, though he had no idea when he would see her again, if at all.

The next day was pretty bad. More than once, he had to quell the powerful impulse to whip out his phone and call her—or worse, to jump in his pickup and go looking for her.

He didn't do it.

A man had his pride, after all.

Van knew she needed to put up or shut up— to actually talk to Jameson, try to work it out with him, however that might end up going. Or to leave him alone.

Working it out, though? The thought simply paralyzed her.

Because she'd tried to work it out so many times in her life before. And every time, she ended up messed over and left behind. Maybe for once, she should try a different way.

They'd agreed where this was going when they started in together. She'd wanted it to last until the end of August.

But she needed to face facts here. The longer she let it go on, the more she would suffer when it ended.

All that day, she waffled between letting last night be their final night and simply staying away—or going to him, trying to talk to him, to explain to him, to somehow get him to see that she needed to walk away now, that sticking through another month would only make it harder to say goodbye.

Explaining herself to him—or just disappearing. Both options seemed weak and wrong and selfish. Probably because both options were all three of those things.

Around five, alone in the apartment with Callie still at work, Van made her decision. She would stay away. He deserved better than to have to deal with her baggage and excuses.

Ten minutes later, she grabbed her keys and ran out the door.

* * *

Feeling pretty damn low, Jameson sat on the front step with Slim. As he watched the cottony clouds roll by in the wide, blue sky, he kept thinking he ought to drag himself inside, find something for dinner.

So far, he hadn't budged an inch.

"Come on, boy. Let's rustle up some grub."

He was just about to get up and go inside when Vanessa's Subaru came flying over the last ridge on the access road from the highway. Kicking up dust devils, the silver SUV raced right for him. When she turned into his driveway, she hit the brakes hard, spun the wheel and sent a wild spray of dirt and pebbles flying in the air behind her.

Slamming to a stop inches from the garage door, she jumped from the car and ran around the back end of the vehicle as he rose to his height from his perch on the step. Beside him, Slim let out a whine that might have been a greeting but sounded more like pure apprehension.

"Stay, boy," he said low. "It's okay."

Slim plunked his haunches back down as she strode up the front walk.

Stopping a few feet from him and the dog, she dragged in a big breath, swiped a wild curl of hair out of her eyes and announced, "All right. I get that we really do have to talk."

"Come on inside." He spoke softly, soothingly,

the way he would to a nervous filly. Turning, he pulled open the door for her.

She marched past him into the foyer. He ushered Slim in behind her and took up the rear. She only got as far as the grouping of oversize sofas and easy chairs around the fireplace. Halting beside the low, long coffee table, she knelt to greet Slim, who dropped to his butt and sat looking up at her hopefully as she stroked his forehead and rubbed his skinny back.

"Right here is fine." She gave Slim one last pat on the head and then rose.

With a low whine, his tail dragging a little, Slim headed for his water bowl. Even the dog knew something bad was happening.

As Slim lapped up water by the counter in the kitchen, Jameson gestured toward a chair. "Let's sit down."

"No, thanks." She stuck her hands in her pockets, her eyes not quite meeting his. "I'll stand."

Judging by the frantic look of misery on her face and the rigid set of her shoulders, he didn't hold out a lot of hope for whatever she planned to say—and that made his gut twist in a knot. She hadn't even dumped him yet, and already he was feeling the pain.

Desperate to make the moment go in a better direction, he said, "I've got an idea…"

She blinked. Apparently, she hadn't banked on

him making suggestions before she finished telling him goodbye. "I, um, what?"

"Let's go out, you and me. Right now. We'll have dinner at DJ's Deluxe or that great French place, Coeur de l'Ouest. If you're in the mood for casual, we can get pizza or stop in at Bronco Burgers. It doesn't matter where we go, just that we do it. Let's walk out of here together and go where we want to go and not hide away here like we're some dirty secret."

Those frantic eyes looked as if they might bug right out of her head. "What are you talking about? We've been through this. You said you understood."

"No. I never said that. I don't understand. I want to be with you, so I did things your way. But your way isn't working. It's time we changed things up. Time you got past whatever's holding you back. You're not eighteen, with a cheating ex-boyfriend and a bunch of mean girls on your ass. You're not dealing with Don or David or Chaz or Trevor. You're with me, and I want to be with you. You are a brilliant, beautiful, grown-up woman, and I think, if you would just get out of your own damn way, you would see that you want to be with me, too."

"No. You're not listening. You refuse to see. I'm not going out openly with you in this town. I can't do that, and you know I can't."

He answered with a sad shake of his head. "Come on, Vanessa. We both know you damn well *can* go out with me tonight. You just *won't*, and that's the plain truth."

Now she looked a little less frantic and a lot more miserable. Her rigid shoulders slumped. "Okay. You're right. I *won't*. That's what I came here to tell you. I considered just staying away, but that felt all wrong."

"And this, what you're doing now—that's somehow *right*?"

"It is right. It's the right choice for me."

"Wrong."

She pressed her lips together and glared at him. "Will you let me finish?"

He returned her glare. "You go right ahead."

"I just… I realized I needed to say it straight to your face, Jameson. Because this isn't anything against you, it really isn't. You are the most amazing man and it's not—"

"Wait. Are you about to hit me with some tired phrase that women always use when they show a guy the door? Are you about to say that it's not me, it's you? If you are, save it. I don't need to hear that crap. I know it without your saying it. Because it *is* you. If we don't work this out, that's on you. I'm knocking myself out here to get through to you, and you're giving me nothing but arguments that don't hold water and a bunch of lame excuses."

"I just... I can't..." She caught herself. "I mean, I *won't*. I won't go there again. I won't take that chance again. I just need to face reality here. It never goes well. It's always a disaster. *I'm* a disaster, romantically speaking." Her wonderful face was a portrait in pain.

His growing exasperation melted away. He wanted to comfort her, but he knew she wouldn't allow him to get one step closer than where he stood now, ten feet from her, at the end of a long gray sofa.

Again, he tried to get her to reason it out. "It's what life is, Vanessa. You fail and fail and every time you fail, you have to pick yourself up and try again. You can't give up—or you'll never succeed."

"It's just not the same for you. You failed once. I just keep doing it over and over. It always has a bad ending for me, and I have to learn to protect myself at least a little. The way I see it, if we walk away now, at least we have a great memory of how good it was for a while."

He hardly knew where to go with that. "But why walk away when we're just getting started? Why walk away when we could have so much more? I've got no intention of messing this up. I want to be with you. I'm open to you. I want it all with you. I want to take this thing between us wherever it goes. I love—"

"Stop. Right there." Her face had paled, her freckles standing out in sharp relief.

How could he get through to her if she refused to hear the words? "You're not even going to let me say it?"

"No, I am not. There's no point in saying it. It won't change anything. You know where it goes. We've been through this. In August, I go back to Billings and we both get on with our lives."

"Just, please, give it a chance between us, Vanessa." Damn. He'd descended to begging. This was bad. Really bad. Still, he gave it one more shot. "Just say yes to dinner at DJ's. That's all I'm asking for. One step at a time."

She made a strangled sound, a sound full of pain. Behind her black-framed glasses, her eyes gleamed with moisture. A tear got away from her and dribbled down the curve of her cheek. Angrily, she swiped at it. "I can't. I'm sorry. No."

No.

And where did that leave him?

Screwed, that's where. "So I guess that makes me collateral damage once again, huh? You said it and I agreed with you. This really *isn't* about me. This is on you, Vanessa. And I'm tired. I'm done. I don't want to give up on you. But what else can I do? A man needs to know when to call it quits."

"Yes." Her voice was so small, so lonely. "You're right. It's not going to work, and it's good that you can see that."

They stared at each other.

There was nothing more to say.

He walked away from her, to the kitchen area and the wide window with a view of the mountains, their craggy peaks reaching into the sky. "Just go," he said over his shoulder.

"Goodbye, Jameson." The words came out ragged but way too damned determined. He heard her footsteps retreating. The front door opened and clicked shut.

He refused to turn from the window until he knew she'd gone. His soul ached at the sound of her car starting up, the engine revving as she shifted and backed out. Finally, she must have put it in Drive. He heard the faint sounds of tires crunching gravel. He stared at the faraway mountains as the sound of her engine faded away.

Behind him, Slim whined. To Jameson, that whine—forlorn, bewildered—said it all.

He turned and met Slim's worried eyes. "It's okay, boy," he lied. It was not in any way okay. "We did what we could."

Slim followed him over to the long gray sofa. The dog sat and stared up at him through sad, soulful eyes. Dropping to the cushions, Jameson put his head in his hands. With another mournful whine, Slim rested his head on Jameson's knees.

Chapter Eleven

Van got home before Callie. She went straight to her room and threw herself across her bed.

She cried for over an hour, stopping now and then to blot her streaming eyes and blow her nose—only to start sobbing all over again.

Finally, Callie tapped on her door and asked apprehensively, "Van?"

She considered trying to tell her friend she was fine. But it would be a flat out lie, a lie that Callie wouldn't buy, anyway. And Van desperately needed the comfort her friend would give her—comfort she knew she didn't really deserve.

She grabbed the tissue box again. Too bad it

was empty. With a low moan, she called, "It's not locked!"

Callie pushed open the door enough to poke her head through. Her pretty face fell. "Oh, honey. What's happened?"

Van cast a sad glance at the pile of used tissues in drifts all around her and held out the box. "I broke up with Jabesud, ad I'b all out of tissues."

"Oh, sweetie…" Callie came to her, swept a pile of tissues off the bed, dropped down beside her and wrapped her in a hug.

Half an hour later, Callie coaxed her into the kitchen and pulled out a stool for her at the counter. "Sit. This calls for tomato soup and a grilled cheese sandwich."

Van blew her nose with a tissue from the fresh box Callie had found in the hall cupboard. "I'm not hungry."

"Too bad. Tomato soup and grilled cheese are what Dr. Sheldrick ordered. You will sit there and take your medicine, are we clear?"

"Ugh. Fine."

Callie whipped up the comfort food and served them both at the counter.

"Thank you," muttered Van after she'd savored the first gooey bite of grilled perfection.

Now Callie looked at her sternly. "I love you a lot. But you've made a giant mistake breaking up with that man."

Van sipped a spoonful of soup. "Noted. Can we talk about something else now?"

Callie changed the subject, and Van loved her all the more for letting it go. Later, they streamed a movie and shared a giant bowl of popcorn.

In the morning, Van got up and went to Happy Hearts. She kept it together, getting through the day's workshop, hanging around afterward to muck stalls and groom horses, mostly sweet old nags who would no longer be breathing if Daphne hadn't provided them a loving place to live out their twilight years.

"Stay for dinner," Daphne urged when Van came in from the stables. "The family is coming." She meant Wanda, Grandma Daisy and Winona, not the Taylors. The situation between Daphne and her dad had not improved.

Van started to decline the invitation, but why? It wasn't as though she had somewhere else to be. Callie didn't need to spend another evening babysitting her. This way, she would have a reason to keep a smile on her face—either that, or she would have to get honest with the people she loved.

No. Never mind honesty. They didn't need to hear how she'd gotten way too serious about a Bronco man. They wouldn't understand her original plan anyway, how it was all supposed to be fun and casual, something she could easily walk away from. And then she'd gone and let her heart get involved and so had he—which meant she'd had to end it a month early.

None of that would make a lick of sense to them.

Really, would it make any sense to anyone? When she laid it all out like that, she just felt like a fool on top of having a broken heart—one she'd inflicted upon herself.

No.

She would be cheerful and upbeat, and none of them would ever have to know.

It didn't go quite as Van planned. She tried to keep her attitude light and easy, but the family knew that something had gone wrong for her. They each found an opportunity to speak to her privately, to ask what she had on her mind and reassure her they were there for her any time she needed them.

In response, she hugged them and said that she loved them and lied through her teeth, promising she was totally fine.

She felt bad about the lying.

But then her mom took her aside last. It was just the two of them, at the kitchen table.

Wanda asked softly, "Are you happy, sweetheart?"

And it was too much. Van couldn't bring herself to tell one more lie. "I'm doing my best, okay? Just putting one foot in front of the other."

"Is that really enough for you?"

"Of course not. But it's where I am right now—and please don't start in about how I need to find a nice local guy and move back home. I like my life in Billings. It's a good life." And it was. Still, her heart ached to think of returning to her pretty little condo in August. Somehow now, after Jameson, the thought of going back to Billings felt hollow at the core.

Her mom took her hand, turned it over, and gently stroked her palm. "I know you've made a good life there. And, yes, I do wish that you would decide to move home. But that's your decision. I promise I'm not trying to live your life for you."

"Well, I just don't think you approve of my choices."

"That's not so, honey. I don't always agree with you, true. But I admire you. You're a terrific teacher. You have a big heart. You're generous with your time and talents and you've made a meaningful, productive life for yourself. I respect your right to do things your own way."

Van felt ashamed. "Thanks, Mom. I did really think you were judging me."

"I'm not. *We're* not."

Van sagged in her chair and said in a small

voice, "I'm sorry if I jumped to conclusions. Over the years, though, you and Grandma Daisy *have* gotten on me now and then about how much happier I would be in Bronco."

"We love you. We want you close. And you're right, your grandma and I have made it painfully clear we wish you would move home. I promise you, though, we do get that it's your decision where you live, *how* you live. As long as you're happy with your choices, we're happy too."

Van told her mom the truth. "Well, I'm not all that happy right at the moment. Does that mean you're going to start in on me to move back here?"

Her mother's laugh was soft and knowing. "Not a chance. I am getting your message loud and clear and I will take it to heart, I promise you. Yes, I want you happy. But I do understand that I can't *give* you happiness. You have to claim it for yourself."

"So where does that leave us?"

"Hmm. That leaves me telling you again that I respect your choices. And that I'm here for you whenever you need me."

They gazed at each other for the longest time. Van was the one to scoot her chair closer to Wanda's. She laid her head on her mother's shoulder with a sigh. "I love you, Mom."

Her mother's arm was warm, comforting around her. "And I love you…"

* * *

Back at the apartment, Callie met her at the door. One look at her friend's determined expression and Van longed to spin on her heel and get out of there.

"This way," said Callie. She took Van by the arm, led her to the sofa in the living area and gently pushed her down. "I realize I didn't come on strong enough with you about the Jameson situation."

"Wait. What? Strong enough?" Where was shy, unassuming Callie when Van needed her? Ordinarily, Van loved that her friend always told her the truth. Right now, though? No, thanks. "Callie, I told you, there *is* no Jameson situation."

Callie braced her hands on her hips. "Denial is not a good look on you."

"I really don't want to talk about this."

"Great. You don't have to talk. Just sit there and listen. Let me say what I need to say, and then we can leave it alone."

With a heart-heavy sigh, Van slumped into the couch cushions. "Get it over with, then."

"Thank you." Callie dropped down next to Van and shifted to face her. "I just want you think about it. Think about how Jameson treats you, how much he wants to be with you. I think, if you just push your fears aside and look at what he *does*, how he *communicates*, all the ways he treats you thoughtfully, with real care, you will see that he's nothing like the men who hurt you."

"Callie. Those guys were all good to me, too. At first."

"As good as Jameson?"

Van hated that question. It had her thinking of all the ways Jameson treated her right. Cooking meals for both of them, rearranging his schedule to be with her, planning weekend getaways—to a secluded cabin with all the amenities, to a luxury hotel—getaways that followed her rules of no contact with anyone else in Bronco.

"Okay," she muttered darkly. "The man's a real prize. So far. But that doesn't mean he would stay that way if I hung around."

"What it means is that you need to give the guy a chance."

"You know how many times you've said I should give Jameson a chance?"

Callie scoffed. "Not enough times, apparently. Because you're still not hearing me."

"Oh, but I do hear you, loud and clear. I hear you and I simply refuse to go there. I will not give my heart again and end up getting it back in pieces."

Callie seemed to be running out of steam. She gave it one more valiant push. "Truly, Van, you know you have to keep trying. Not all men are like your dad and those other four losers whose names I don't even want mentioned ever again. You'll never get what matters if you give up now."

"Then I'll never get what matters."

Callie let out a dejected little moan. "You are just making me so sad."

Van took both her hands. "You are the best friend ever. I love that you're trying so hard to convince me to do what you think is right. It just, well, it isn't right for me. And I have to do what works for me."

Callie hung her head.

Van pulled her close in a hug. "Thank you. I mean that." She took her friend by the shoulders and held her away enough to capture her gaze. "Now, can we stop talking about this. Please?"

"All right." Callie gave a weary nod. "I've said what I needed to say and you're still dug in. I give up. Have it your way."

Callie kept her word. Over the next few days, she never once mentioned Jameson.

Too bad Van thought of him constantly. And she remembered everything Callie had said, damn it. She couldn't stop thinking of all the ways he'd shown her how much he cared. And she couldn't stop missing him, stop reaching for him in the middle of the night.

But she didn't take her friend's advice. She

stayed away from him. Her fear of getting hurt again had more power than her longing to make things right.

On Wednesday, the third day after Vanessa dumped him, Jameson woke before dawn to the sound of the doorbell ringing. He almost pulled the covers over his head and went back to sleep, but it was time for him to get up and get to work, anyway.

The doorbell chimed again as he stuck his feet in his jeans, zipped up and pulled on an old Grizzlies sweatshirt. "I'm coming! Hold your horses!"

With Slim at his bare heels, he headed for the door.

It was his mom. "Hey." He put on a smile. "You're out and about early."

She folded her arms across her middle and tilted her chin high. "Chicken-fried steak tonight. It's your all-time favorite, and I am frying it up for you. We never see you. Tonight you are coming for dinner. Be there. Six o'clock." She didn't wait for a reply, but turned on her boot heel, ran down the steps, jumped into the old pickup she often used around the property and drove off.

He didn't want to go. He just wanted to work and be left the hell alone. But once roused to action over one of her children, Mimi John wouldn't quit. If he didn't show up tonight, she would march back over here, Dawson and Maddox in tow. And when she ordered his brothers to drag him bodily to the main house right this instant, they would do it, no questions asked.

Bottom line on this issue: he would end up at dinner with the family whether he wanted to go or not.

He went. At least he got chicken-fried steak with country gravy and buttery, light-as-a-cloud mashed potatoes for his trouble.

All three of his siblings showed up. Charity sat next to him. When she thought no one was paying attention, she whispered, "Everything all right, big brother?"

"Sure. Yeah. Fine."

"I should talk to her..."

He looked at her dead-on. "Don't."

She gave him the sad eyes, but she left it alone after that.

A few minutes later, his dad said, "Jameson, we haven't seen that silver Subaru over at your place the past few days. Everything all right?"

Jameson gave his dad the same look he'd given his sister—the one that said Randall should drop that subject now.

His dad pretended not to get the memo. "A man can't be sitting around waiting for what he wants to come to him. He's got to go out and go after what's his."

Jameson glared at the spot between his father's bushy gray eyebrows. "Dad. I mean it. Don't."

His family knew better than this—and no, he wasn't surprised they'd all noticed the absence of Vanessa's car in his driveway. Of course, they all knew that he'd been seeing Vanessa. Nothing got by any of them. But as a rule, they had the good sense not to butt in on his business.

His mother settled the matter by chiding mildly, "Randall, let it be." And then she changed the subject. "How's the gravy, Jameson?"

He gave his mom a slow nod. "The best. Thanks, Mom."

The rest of the dinner went by without incident in that no one else tried to bring up the sudden absence of Vanessa from his life. He really didn't want to talk about her.

Too bad not talking about her didn't stop him from thinking of her all the time. He conjured images of her at Happy Hearts leading her Young Adventurers in some new science experiment. He kept remembering her face at the moment she won the Miss Bronco crown, so horrified and absolutely adorable, spitting a giant bite of pie all over her old T-shirt and jeans. Even pissed off on behalf of his sister, he'd thought Vanessa was about the cutest, most bewildered Miss Bronco he'd ever seen.

He loved the way she treated Slim, always taking time to greet the mutt properly, give him a good scratch around the neck as she let him lick her face. She asked Slim how he was feeling and then listened as if he actually answered her in English. Vanessa was the kind who always made sure Slim got plenty of kibble. She took him out to do his business any time he whined at the door.

Slim missed her. The sound of a vehicle driving by out front would have him racing to the door. Plunking his butt down, staring hopefully at that shut door, Slim would wait for her to come through it.

Since Sunday, she never did.

For Jameson, nights without her were the worst of all. He woke often with his hand stretched out into the cool expanse of sheet where her lush, soft body damn well belonged.

He needed to do something, change something, make a move.

But he couldn't think of any move that would get through to her, help her to see the light, get her to accept that he loved her and wanted to be with her. That she was the one for him, that he was all hers, the man different from all the others, the one who would never let her down.

Thursday morning, he remembered he hadn't picked up the mail in a while. He drove out to the mailbox and gathered the stack of bills and flyers and worthless junk. Back at the house, he tossed his keys on the kitchen table and went through the envelopes and advertising circulars, tossing most of it in a pile to discard.

At the bottom of the stack, he found a flyer for Winona Cobbs's new psychic enterprise. Printed on deep purple cardstock with bright yellow lettering, the flyer announced that Winona could be consulted at her new shop, Wisdom by Winona, located on the premises of Bronco Ghost Tours.

Life! Love! Happiness! the flyer proclaimed in giant shouty yellow caps. The flyer announced that consultations, consolation and excellent advice could all be attained in a visit with Winona.

Jameson stared at that flyer for a good five minutes. For half that time, he was shaking his head. He admired Winona, but that didn't mean he would ever waste good money on a visit to a fortune teller.

He tossed the flyer on top of the junk mail stack—and then snatched it right up again. Sticking it in a back pocket, he scooped up his keys from where he'd thrown them on the table and headed for the door.

At Bronco Ghost Tours, he found that Winona had her own separate building. The discovery brought relief that he wouldn't have to go near the office or the gift shop, where he might run into Vanessa's roommate or even her brother, Evan.

It was something of a shed really, Winona's

shop—a very charming wooden shed. Painted turquoise, the rough plank siding had been decorated with stars and crescent moons. Wisdom by Winona, announced the sign above the heavy purple door. To either side of that door, thick curtains covered the old-fashioned double-hung windows. He couldn't see anything inside.

Jameson stood on the step for a few minutes, growing more and more unsure that he had any right to be here. Really, seeking out Vanessa's great-grandmother could end up being just as awkward as meeting up with Callie or Evan.

In fact, the more he considered going through that purple door, the more certain he became that showing up here was a bad idea. Better to just get out. He turned for his quad cab—and heard the door open behind him.

"Jameson John," said a husky voice with only the slightest quaver of age.

Slowly, he turned back to face her. "Winona. Hello."

Wizened and bright-eyed as ever, Winona wore an outfit worthy of his ex-wife, the rodeo queen, including purple jeans, boots to match and a jewel-bedecked purple shirt. On her head she wore a purple turban accented with an enormous gold brooch in the shape of a crescent moon.

"About time you came to see me." With a gleeful little laugh, Winona reached out her skinny, wrinkled hand and grabbed his arm. "Don't dally on the step, young man. Come in, come in. We need to get moving on this."

This, what? he would have asked, if only his throat hadn't suddenly locked up tight.

A moment later, he found himself on the other side of the door. Winona gave that door a push. It swung shut, and semidarkness descended. The only light came from dim bulbs in ancient-looking lamps. Jameson breathed in the heavy scent of incense. It burned in several brass containers set on small tables next to faded wing chairs.

Apparently, this was some kind of waiting room—a very purple waiting room almost completely enclosed in purple velvet curtains. Anchored in the center of the ceiling, the curtains draped outward to the top of the walls. From there, except for where they parted above the door, they hung straight to the floor.

"Winona." He had to pause to clear his throat. "This is very, er, atmospheric."

The old woman glanced around with a grin. "Designed it myself. The older I get, the more I love purple." Her grin flattened out. "Unfortunately, Evan is insisting that I'll have to move indoors. He says we can't possibly keep this sweet little shed warm through a Montana winter." Before he could sympathize with her, she brightened right up again. "All right, then. Let's get started, shall we?" She lifted a hidden split in the curtains, revealing another door that led to a second room. "This way." Ushering him over the threshold first, she followed him in, shutting the door behind them.

He breathed a little easier. No incense burned in this room. And there were no draperies back here, either, just clean walls of a pale, soothing robin's egg blue.

Winona signaled him to take one of the two chairs at a central table of simple bleached pine. "Sit, please."

He sat. Winona perched on the chair across from him.

Feeling nervous as a sinner in church, he coughed into his hand again—and suddenly realized he hadn't taken off his hat. Swiping the thing from his head, he turned to hook it on the back of the chair.

When he faced Winona again, her piercing dark eyes watched him, seeming to see right to the center of him. Did she find him lacking somehow? "I, uh, always enjoyed that column of yours."

"Thank you." She reached across the table and took his wrist. "Down to business." Turning his hand palm up, she cradled it in her birdlike claw. Bending her turbaned head close, she hummed low in her throat. "Hmm…"

Alarm jangled through him. "What is it? What's wrong?"

She glanced up, sharp eyes pinning him again. And then her face softened. Her voice changed, became gentle, soothing. "Let's just sit quietly, shall we?"

He longed to leap up and run out, but he heard himself answer calmly, "Sure." As he said the word, his urge to run faded. A sort of peacefulness stole through him.

They sat. Minutes ticked by. He felt truly unconcerned, relaxed, certain now that something good would happen. He only needed to be patient, to let the truth unfold at its own chosen pace.

Gently, Winona touched the tips of his fingers one by one. She bent even closer and stared at his open palm.

Again, she made that humming sound.

"Hmm… It appears to me, Jameson, that you are the kind of man who likes to take charge. You don't care for ambiguity, and you do not like to wait." She glanced up, and their gazes locked. "Has there ever been a time when you didn't get what you wanted?"

He took a while to consider her question. "When I was younger, no. Things came easily to me back then."

She chuckled. The small, spare room seemed to fill with light. "You've led a charmed life?"

He glanced around, trying to figure out where the extra light had come from. There were windows on three of the walls, each with white lace curtains drawn shut, letting muted light in that didn't seem to have gotten brighter. And the two lamps on side tables gave about the same amount of light as before. Still, the room did seem brighter.

Winona shook a finger at him. "Pay attention, please, Jameson."

He blinked and sat up straighter. "Sorry, ma'am."

"Answer my question."

"About my so-called charmed life?"

Winona beamed. "That's the one."

"Ahem. Well, yeah. Looking back, I'd have to say that I've had it really good."

"Until...?"

"I got married. It didn't work out. We divorced. She moved away. I felt disappointed in myself, you know? That I never really understood her. And then, once she was gone, I didn't even miss her all that much. I started to wonder if there was something missing in *me*. If I would ever find someone to be my one. To be my only."

Winona held his gaze again. "There is nothing missing in you, Jameson."

Hope rose like a bubble in his chest. He swallowed. Hard. "There's not?"

"Nope." She popped the *p*, looking almost

childlike at that moment. "You're on the right path. Patience is required, though. You can't have what you want until the one you want is ready."

"Before she left…" He realized he should clarify. "I mean the one I want. Not my ex-wife."

Winona's smile turned serene. "I know what you mean."

Did she? He really had no idea. But in this quiet, bright little room, just Winona and him, alone, well, it seemed like the right choice to take her at her word. "I started to tell her how I really feel for her. I wanted to let her know what's in my heart…"

Winona said nothing. She waited for him to finish.

He did. "Because I love her."

"But you *didn't* tell her?"

"No."

"You changed your mind?"

He shook his head. "She wouldn't let me say it—and I let her stop me. I shouldn't have let her do that. I should've said it anyway."

Winona touched his curled-up fingertips again, and he relaxed them until they opened as before. "Timing matters," she said. "That might seem wrong. It might even seem unfair. But sometimes, there's no point in saying your love out loud if the one you love can't hear you yet."

"I don't know about that."

Winona lifted one narrow shoulder in a tiny shrug. "Think on it."

"I will." He stared into the old woman's eyes. And the truth just popped out. "It's Vanessa. I'm in love with Vanessa." There. Finally. He'd said it. And it felt damn good to say it, so he said it again. "I love your great-granddaughter."

Winona granted him an angel's smile. "Yes. I know."

Huh? That made no sense at all. "I don't understand. Vanessa said she didn't want her family to know about us. I'm surprised that she told you."

"She didn't. Vanessa never said a word. But I have spent many years watching and learning. Sometimes the secrets of the heart are open to me. I simply *know* things—secret things, the things we all try to hide about ourselves. That first time I met you, at the barbecue on Independence Day, I knew then that you were already falling in love with my great-granddaughter. And the moment I looked in your blue eyes today, Jameson, I knew that it had happened, that you *are* in love with Vanessa."

He had no idea what to say to that. Maybe no words were necessary. After all, Winona clearly had him pegged.

She said, "Sometimes I know the deepest secrets, the ones in people's hearts, the ones they haven't even shared with themselves. For instance, Vanessa…"

He leaned in, eager for anything the old woman might share. "Yes, what? Tell me."

Winona lowered her voice to a whisper. "Vanessa's been hurt. Love hasn't been kind to her."

"I know that. She told me."

"She told you because, deep in her wounded heart, she *does* trust you. And she's hiding the truth from herself. But that doesn't make it any less true."

"Whoa. Slow down a second there. What truth are you talking about?"

"Why, that she's in love with you, too."

Should that news have surprised him? It didn't. He believed that Vanessa loved him—and that loving him scared the hell out of her. What he needed to do next to get through to her, that was the real question.

"And you must be patient," Winona said.

"Yeah," he replied glumly. "You mentioned that already."

"Patient and available, too."

"Oh, come on, Winona. How can I be available when she's already dumped me?"

"Find your opportunities. She misses you."

He shouldn't get his hopes up, but Winona could be so damn convincing. His pulse quickening, he sat up straighter. "You're sure about that?"

"Yes. She loves you and she misses you, she

absolutely does. So show up. Let her see exactly what she's missing."

"Winona, even if I could get her to agree to be with me again, it wouldn't be for real, you know? She doesn't want anyone in town to know about us. And I went along with that for a while, I did. But enough is enough. I just don't want to be a secret anymore."

"Of course you don't. And you shouldn't have to be."

"So, how do I make *her* see that?"

"Patience. Don't stay away just because she insists on terms you can't accept—but don't push, either. She has to come to you in her own time."

He let out a groan. "You don't ask much, do you?"

"Jameson, you have to lose in order to win."

"Winona, what does that even mean?"

For that he got her most beatific smile. "All will become clear. In time. Right now, you need to show up. Your very presence will serve to remind her of all that's at stake."

"Show up where? Are you saying I should stalk her?"

"Of course not. There will always be opportunities for you to be where she is."

"Right," he said bleakly.

"Don't descend into cynicism," Winona warned gently. "Love is on the line, Jameson. Above all, you mustn't give up the fight."

Chapter Twelve

The next day, Saturday, Van and Callie were sitting at the kitchen counter sipping second cups of coffee at eight in the morning when the doorbell rang.

"I'll get it." Van got up and went to answer. A glance through the peephole showed her Charity John's smiling face. She pulled the door wide to find Jameson's sister, resplendent in dress jeans and a gorgeous Western shirt, clutching the handle of her makeup kit. "Just thought I'd drop by in case you could use a little extra primping for the ribbon cutting today." The newly remodeled Bronco Convention Center had its grand opening that morning at ten. Miss Bronco was slated to do the honors.

"It's so good to see you." Van stepped back. "Come in."

Charity entered the narrow entry hallway. Van shut the door and grabbed her in a quick hug, one made awkward by the case caught between them. "How 'bout some coffee?"

"Yes, please."

There were only two stools at the counter, so the three of them sat at the table for a while. At eight thirty, Callie left to run errands, promising to see them both at the ribbon cutting.

"I bought some dressy shirts and hats," Van reported. She led Charity down the hall to her room, took her new Miss Bronco wardrobe from the closet and laid the various pieces out on the bed.

"I love them," the younger woman declared. She fingered the sleeve of one of the shirts. "I think this bronze color is amazing, and I love the gold beading. It's perfect for your skintone. You can wear the chocolate-brown studded jeans with it, the dark boots and dark hat with the gold-colored crystal beading."

Van put the other pieces back in the closet.

"Let me do your makeup, just like old times," said Charity.

Van laughed. "Old times meaning four weeks ago?"

Charity grabbed her in another hug. "I've missed you," she whispered.

"I've missed you, too." Van took her hand. "All right. Enough with the hugfest. Let's get to work."

In the bathroom, Charity plunked the makeup kit on the counter. She took off Van's glasses, tipped up her chin and studied her face. "Your eyes are a little red."

She hadn't been sleeping. Her bed just felt so empty without Jameson beside her. "The contacts have been bothering me," she lied.

"You have eye drops?"

"Of course."

"Use them. And I think you should wear glasses today."

"Miss Bronco in glasses?" Van put on a snooty voice. "Is that done?"

"*You* are Miss Bronco, and you wear glasses— so the answer is yes. It is most definitely done. I think those tortoiseshell ones will look best with that gorgeous shirt…" Charity's voice trailed off. She seemed to gather her courage.

"What is it?" Van demanded.

"I just need to say something. Please don't cut me off."

Van drew a long breath. "All right. Go ahead."

"You could have everything. You're so smart

and you are loved, Vanessa." Tears filled her eyes. "I don't know what went wrong between you and my brother, but I do know that whatever it is, you can fix it. You can make it right. I know him. You can trust him. He will never, ever mess you over." Charity pulled a tissue from her pocket and dabbed gently at her eyes.

"Okay." She gave a delicate little sniffle. "That's it, all I needed to say to you—I mean, except that, no matter what happens, I really want us to still be friends."

"Always," Van vowed, as it came to her that her deepest hurts were truly healing, in no small part due to her friendship with Charity. "And I..."

Charity looked at her through hopeful, shining eyes. "Yes? Oh, Vanessa. Whatever it is, you can tell me."

Could she?

She went for it. "The truth is, I have been thinking about Jameson. Constantly. And Charity, you are so right. He's a good man, the best. And I do need to let my old hurts go."

Charity nodded hard. "You need to make room in your heart. Room for happiness."

"I do."

"But..." Charity's smooth brown crinkled. "What hurts are we talking about here, exactly?"

Van gave a tiny shrug. "Well, for starters, disappointments in love. There have been a lot of those in my life so far."

"Jameson won't be one of those guys. He knows how special you are. I meant what I said a minute ago. Jameson will not let you down."

"I know he won't." Van felt strangely breathless. She'd blown it with him. She really had. She'd been too busy protecting her wounded heart to let him in. "He's different. I know it. You're right about that, too."

Charity took both her hands. "I really think you two are meant to be together."

Van couldn't suppress a chuckle. "You're such a romantic."

Charity drew her slim shoulders back. "I am, and proud of it—and don't stop now. Tell me what other past hurts are bothering you."

Van confessed, "Well, in my life there have been some extremely mean girls."

Charity groaned. "Ugh. The mean girls. They're the worst. You have to stand up to them, show them they won't get you down."

"You're right. And I did. And it was a long, long time ago. Long enough that there's no excuse for me not to get past it. Luckily for me, now I have you and Callie and Daphne. Good women and wonderful friends with open minds and big hearts. I feel so grateful for you and for them."

"Oh, Vanessa!" Charity cried, grabbing her in another, tighter hug. "I feel grateful for you, too."

It all seemed so clear suddenly. She'd judged her hometown by the heartbreak she'd suffered in high school. She'd run away and refused to return except for short family visits—because of a boy she'd trusted with everything who then threw her away, because of a group of jealous, vindictive high school girls.

But already, from last Christmas through this summer, she'd forged some wonderful relationships with terrific women right here in Bronco. She'd met Jameson, a man she knew she could count on, even as she refused to let herself trust him. She needed to stop blaming her hometown for Donnie's betrayal and the vindictiveness of Maura and her crew.

She needed to be braver. Truer. To be more like the Bronco women she loved—open, authentic, full of love and understanding, proud to step up and live their convictions.

"What?" Charity took Van's face between her slender hands. "You look stunned. Are you okay? Did what I said upset you?"

"Upset me? No! I'm good. Really, I am. As a matter of fact, I feel better than I've felt in a long time." Even the ever-present ache of loss that had dragged at her since she'd walked out Jameson's door last Sunday had somehow lessened, at least a little. "And what you said about Jameson, I *was* listening. I really was. And I know you're right. He's a fine man. The best. I promise to take what you said to heart."

Charity stroked Van's hair. "I'm glad." She hugged Van again. "Anytime you need someone to talk to, I'm here for you. I hope you know that."

"I do. And thank you. You know I'm here for you, too."

Charity beamed. "Yes, I do." She turned to her makeup case. "All right. Let's get you ready to wow them at the ribbon cutting."

Charity had plans with her friends for that afternoon, so she and Van drove separate vehicles to the convention center.

When they arrived, the parking lot was already more than half-full. Charity honked and waved Van into the first empty space.

Van parked, jumped out and ran to Charity's side window. "I'm good from here. I'll be watching for you in the crowd."

"I'll be whistling and waving."

Van reached in and squeezed her friend's shoulder. "Thank you. You're the best." She stood for a moment, watching the back end of Charity's cute little pickup until it disappeared down the next row.

Twenty minutes later, she sat in a row of folding chairs on a raised platform erected in front of the new convention center. The mayor and other dignitaries filled the chairs to either side of her. Below the stage, a brass band played a patriotic anthem, and beyond the band, the plaza that surrounded the center was packed with the citizens of Bronco.

All the flags and bunting from Red, White and Bronco had been repurposed to celebrate the dedication of the center. In the distance, the craggy peaks of the mountains pierced the wide blue bowl of the sky. A nice breeze stirred the flags to full, waving glory.

After three rousing Sousa marches, the band took a break, and the speeches began. Van spotted Charity and her parents in the crowd, but she didn't see Jameson. The ever-present ache in her heart intensified.

She needed to make things right with him. She'd messed everything up with her fears and her doubts. And oh, she did miss him so.

Was it too late for them? Had she finally found the right man for her and then destroyed their chance for happiness by walking away?

Right then, over at the podium, the mayor swept out his arm toward the row of folding chairs. "And now, let's give a big Bronco welcome to the little lady chosen to do the honors today. May I introduce our own Miss Bronco,

Vanessa Cruise!" The crowd on the plaza erupted in cheers, whistles and excited applause. "Come on up here, Vanessa, and say a few words."

Vanessa played her part. Rising, she swept off her sparkly hat and gave the crowd a big, whole-hearted Miss Bronco wave.

They clapped all the louder. She felt their acceptance. Some might have mocked her win at first. But she'd slowly won them over by simply being herself and putting her whole heart into the job.

Leaving her hat on the chair, she approached the podium. The mayor tipped his hat to her and stepped back.

She adjusted the mic and began, "Hello, Bronco!" Again, a surge of applause washed over her. She waited for it to die down a little and then parroted the few remarks she'd planned, all about fresh starts and the importance of community, of people supporting each other, working together. At that point, she was supposed to take the giant pair of scissors from the mayor, step to the ribbon and cut it in two.

But in that split second before she turned to accept the scissors, she realized she had more to say. "I've learned so much since becoming Miss Bronco."

She paused for a slow breath. Out on the plaza, you could have heard a feather float toward the ground. She frowned. "Yeah, okay. I admit it. I didn't enter the pageant to win this honor, and there were ten wonderful contestants who did enter, each of whom had every right to feel a little cheated that I ended up with the crown.

"But every one of those contestants has treated me kindly. Every one of them would have made a great Miss Bronco, I have no doubt. However, thanks to my wonderful, brilliant Young Adventurers out at Happy Hearts Animal Sanctuary, here I am." The whistles and shouting and wild clapping started up again, louder than ever.

The second the sound died down a little, she continued, "And I wear the Miss Bronco crown with pride, thanks in great part to the coaching and encouragement of my fabulous runner-up this year, Charity John. Thank you, Charity!" The crowd went wild.

Again, Van picked up as soon as the wave of sound leveled off. "I know I'm not a traditional beauty queen, but every woman has beauty within her, and none of us should be afraid to let the world see what we know and feel inside." Her voice died in her throat.

But her heart took wings.

Because right then, she saw him—saw Jameson, way back from the platform, working his way toward the front of the crowd. His eyes...they were only for her, locked on her so intently. He wore a look of great tenderness, one that seemed to speak straight to her heart, to say it was far from over between them, after all.

Her vision blurred. Careful of her makeup, she lifted her glasses enough to dash the tears away. And then, drawing her shoulders back, aiming her chin high, Van spoke her truth out loud and proud. "I have known heartbreak. Way too much heartbreak. And this summer, in Bronco, you all have taught me how to get over it—not by hiding what I feel, but by sharing it. I've been so afraid to lose my heart again…" She paused, half expecting the mayor to grab her arm and drag her away from the podium.

Nobody moved. The mayor made not a peep. Out on the plaza, the crowd that seemed to contain everyone in town watched her through wide, rapt eyes.

"However," she said, her gaze locked with Jameson's as he kept moving closer, "sometimes you have to lose in order to win." Another lightning bolt of understanding struck and she found herself remembering something she'd said to Jameson that day he revealed the sad secrets of his failed marriage. She repeated it now, slowly. Clearly. "And sometimes people hurt each other because they're too busy struggling through their own crap to be careful of the other person's heart. I have done that. Everyone messes up now and then. The real progress happens when we learn from our mistakes."

Again, she paused. She drew a deep breath and pictured G-G's beautiful, wrinkled face. Oh, she could feel it now, Winona's love and approval. Winona would be so proud that she'd finally found her own path.

"So I'm just going to say it, right here, right this minute in front of the whole town." She smiled at the man who'd almost reached the platform now. "I have lost my heart to Jameson John—and I'm finally seeing that loving him is the best thing that could ever have happened to me. Because this time, I've lost my heart to the right man, a man I can count on, a man worthy of my trust."

"Vanessa!" Jameson leaped onto the speaker's platform. "I love you!" he shouted, striding straight for her.

The crowd cheered louder than ever. They whistled and threw their hats in the air as the man she loved swept her into his arms.

"I love you," she said, and he swooped down to claim her mouth with his. They kissed for a long, sweet time, the crowd egging them on with more whistles and catcalls.

When they finally came up for air, she said "I love you so much, Jameson," in barely a whisper. Their kiss had knocked her glasses askew. He carefully settled them more firmly on the bridge of her nose.

Behind them, the mayor took matters into his own hands and cut the ribbon. Not that either Van or Jameson cared.

Holding her close, Jameson dipped his head even closer, close enough to speak directly into her ear. "And I want you to know that I honestly don't care where we live as long as I'm living with you. When you leave at the end of the summer, I'm going with you."

"No need!" She had to shout the words to be heard over the clapping and shouting from the plaza. "I'm ready, Jameson, ready to come home for good. I'm applying for a job at Bronco High. One way or another, I'm going to be living here in our hometown."

"With me." It was an outright demand. "Openly."

"Yes, absolutely. With you, for the whole town to see. I love you so much. I've missed you so terribly."

"Never leave me again." His eyes were blue fire.

"Never," she vowed. "I'm sorry I made you a secret. But your willingness to keep it just between us for a while did give us time, at least, to know that we're meant for each other."

"I agree."

She blinked. "You do?"

"Absolutely," he replied. "I thought it over, back the night of the rodeo, after I turned down your offer at Bushwhacker Creek. I figured out then that I would never get a chance with you if I didn't bend a little."

"So that was you, bending, when you showed up at our table during the barbecue on the Fourth?"

"Yes, it was—and dear God, I love you." He touched her cheek with a gentle hand, causing a riot of glorious sensation to flash like sparks across her skin.

"And I love you," she said yet again. "All my disappointments, all my bad boyfriends, my questionable romantic choices, they led me finally to you. Every time I lost at love, I was only getting closer to finding the real thing. Now, I can't wait to see where the future will take us."

"Together," he said in a rough rumble.

"Always," she promised as he pulled her close for another endless, tender kiss.

* * * * *

*Look for the next book in the new
Harlequin Special Edition continuity
Montana Mavericks:
The Real Cowboys of Bronco Heights*

For His Daughter's Sake

by USA TODAY *bestselling author
Stella Bagwell*

*On sale August 2021 wherever Harlequin
books and ebooks are sold.*

**WE HOPE YOU ENJOYED
THIS BOOK FROM**

**SPECIAL
EDITION**

Believe in love. Overcome obstacles. Find happiness.

Relate to finding comfort and strength in the
support of loved ones and enjoy the journey
no matter what life throws your way.

6 NEW BOOKS AVAILABLE EVERY MONTH!

COMING NEXT MONTH FROM

(H) HARLEQUIN
SPECIAL EDITION

#2851 FOR HIS DAUGHTER'S SAKE
Montana Mavericks: The Real Cowboys of Bronco Heights
by Stella Bagwell

Sweet Callie Sheldrick disarms single dad Tyler Abernathy in ways he can't explain, but the widowed rancher is in no position for courting, and he won't ask Callie to take on another woman's child. The kindest thing he can do is to walk away. Yet doing the "right thing" might end up breaking all three of their hearts...

#2852 THE HORSE TRAINER'S SECRET
Return to the Double C • by Allison Leigh

When Megan Forrester finds herself pregnant, she resolves to raise the baby herself. But when Nick Ventura becomes the architect on a ramshackle Wyoming ranch Megan's helping friends turn into a home, that resolve soon weakens. After all, Nick's the total package—gorgeous, capable and persistent. Not to mention the father of her child! If only she could tell him...

#2853 THE CHEF'S SURPRISE BABY
Match Made in Haven • by Brenda Harlen

A family emergency whisks Erin Napper away before chef Kyle Landry can figure out if they've stirred up more than a one-night stand. Almost a year later, Erin confesses her secret to Kyle: their baby! But the marriage of convenience he proposes? Out of the question. Because settling for a loveless relationship would be like forgetting the most important ingredient of all.

#2854 THEIR TEXAS TRIPLETS
Lockharts Lost & Found • by Cathy Gillen Thacker

Cooper Maitland's nieces were left at the ranch for him, but this cowboy isn't equipped to take on three infants on his own. Jillian Lockhart owes Coop, so she'll help him look after the triplets for now—but recklessly falling in love would be repeating past mistakes. As they care for the girls together, can their guarded hearts open enough to become a family?

#2855 THEIR RANCHER PROTECTOR
Texas Cowboys & K-9s • by Sasha Summers

Skylar Davis is grateful to have her late husband's dog. But the struggling widow can barely keep her three daughters fed, much less a hungry canine. Kyle Mitchell was her husband's best friend and he can't stop himself from rescuing them. But will his exposed secrets ruin any chance they have at building a family?

#2856 ACCIDENTAL HOMECOMING
The Stirling Ranch • by Sabrina York

Danny Diem's life is upended when he inherits a small-town ranch. But learning he has a daughter in need of lifesaving surgery is his biggest shock yet. He'd never gotten over his ex Lizzie Michaels. But her loving strength for their little girl makes him wonder if he's ready to embrace the role he's always run from: *father.*

YOU CAN FIND MORE INFORMATION ON UPCOMING HARLEQUIN TITLES, FREE EXCERPTS AND MORE AT HARLEQUIN.COM.

HSECNM0721

From *New York Times* bestselling author

DIANA PALMER

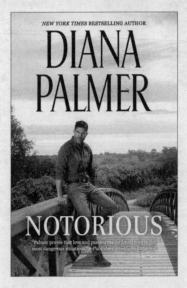

**Trusting him is dangerous.
But resisting him is almost impossible.**

"Palmer proves that love and passion can be found even in the most dangerous situations." —*Publishers Weekly* on *Untamed*

Order your copy today!

HQNBooks.com

PHDPBPA0721